WHEN DARKNESS FALLS

By

KEN HUDNALL

Omega Press
El Paso, Texas

COPYRIGHT 1996 ROBERT K. HUDNALL

ISBN: 0-9754923-8-1

First Edition January 1996
Second Edition October 2004

Omega Press
5823 N. Mesa, #823
El Paso, Texas 79912
Or
http://www.kenhudnall.com

OTHER WORKS BY THE SAME AUTHOR

MANHATTAN CONSPIRACY SERIES
Blood on the Apple
Capital Crimes
Angel of Death
Confrontation

THE OCCULT CONNECTION SERIES
UFOs, Secret Societies and Ancient Gods
The Hidden Race

WHEN DARKNESS FALLS

SPIRITS OF THE BORDER SERIES
(with Connie Wang)
The History and Mystery of El Paso Del Norte
The History and Mystery of Fort Bliss, Texas

PROLOGUE

THE BEGINNING

CHAPTER ONE

Jackson Macabee, the warden, walked slowly into the dimly lit hospital wing. The lowering of the lights was against prison policy, but the chief medical officer insisted that his patients needed sleep. He was acutely aware that the security was less in a hospital surrounding even though located in the prison. Captain Vincent McIntyre, the prison's chief guard, followed Macabee. Waiting for them in front of one of the few isolation rooms was Dr. Amos Martin, the crusty chief surgeon who had been at the prison longer than anyone else.

"How's the patient today?" asked the Warden, glancing at the sheet covered man lying on the bed that filled most of the small room.

Martin shook his shaggy head slowly, "I don't know, physically, he seems fine, those wounds he had seem to have healed quickly, but he's still in a coma."

"How did he come to be in that hidden room?" wondered Captain McIntyre.

"More importantly, who is he?" asked the Warden.

He turned to McIntyre.

"You're sure he's not an inmate. Some of those new one's transferred from the Federal prison at La Tuna could have tried an escape."

McIntyre shook his head and hitched his Sam Brown belt a notch higher.

"No, Warden. I have conducted a thorough check. Everyone one of our prisoners is accounted for. This guy is someone new to the prison."

The Warden shook his head slowly.

"So he is someone who wanted to break in the prison? I find that hard to believe." He said.

The three discussed the injured man for some time, secure in the belief that he was unconscious. However, unknown to them, though he made no move and appeared dead to the world, he heard every word they said. Once he was assured that they meant him no harm, his thoughts flew across the centuries to a time before recorded history; back to a time when gods walked the earth and waged wars against men.

The battle had raged all day, first one army had been victorious and then the other had gained the upper hand. The forces of Asmodeus, the evil one, had fought with unbelievable ferocity, as if secure in the belief that they could not die, a belief fostered by their leader. This total lack of concern for human life had gained the rebels the upper hand in the early days of the Great Civil War, but now, though it still stood them in good stead at isolated parts of the battlefield, the demonic fury was slowly ebbing.

After a long arduous campaign, the forces of Anu had slowly pushed the rebels back to their original starting point, Asmodeus' home city of Etrea In the great Sahara Valley. Now it the rebels turn to feel the brunt of righteous anger as the forces of the Great Lord Anu encircled the city of Etrea, pushing the battered army of the Evil One back against the massive city walls. To their credit, though it was obvious to even the most dedicated of the rebel forces that they faced total destruction, the decimated ranks of Asmodeus' followers showed no sign of fear; fighting fiercely for each foot of ground they were forced to turn over the victors.

On Mount Cerebus, the high ground before the city, the great Lord of Hosts, Anu stood silently, his white robes billowing about him in the errant breeze that did little to disperse the humid heat that added further torment to the warriors below. Anu, the bringer of all that was good to the inhabitants of the planet was a mighty figure, standing almost seven feet tall; his very presence could cow the most ferocious of animals. His eyes could emit radiations that could reduce a human to cinders. But now, this all-powerful being stood with tears streaming down his weathered cheeks. He knew that he was watching the end of all that he and his companions had built on this garden planet.

With great sadness, the mighty figure stared intently across the bloody plain at what had once been a city of unsurpassed beauty. He fleetingly remembered days and nights of bliss visiting the City of Gold, home base for the equally mighty Asmodeus, Anu's own brother of the imperial blood. Now, great pillars of dark smoke towered above the once mighty impenetrable walls. With a sigh, Anu turned from the carnage below him and ponderously walked toward his pavilion running the fingers of his right hand through his long flowing white beard. Though deep in thought, he did notice that his retainers had worked hurriedly to fully erect his command headquarters. He must complement the commander of his guard, he thought.

"Send for my son," he quietly commanded his herald, Apollo, son of his sister.

Absently he returned the salute rendered by the Herald and the two members of his bodyguard who stood like statutes at the entrance of his pavilion.

Entering the cool quietness of the royal enclosure, Anu paused to look around him. One hundred feet wide and over three hundred feet long, he was designed to hold the imperial court. Anu mounted the dais that dominated the center for the great enclosure and seated himself on the great golden throne. He was overcome by incredible sadness at the death and destruction he had witnessed during the campaign. This planet could have been their eternal home, but the civilization they had laboriously built had been brought down by greed and jealousy. Soon they would have to leave.

There was no question in his mind that the paradise the Annunaki had created on this planet was destroyed; hundreds of thousands of his followers were dead and even more of those who followed his wayward brother had died in the long civil war. All this caused by the greed of one who had been so close to him. So much that they had built over the centuries was gone.

The entrance of his son roused him from his musings. He watched with some pride as his tall, strong son halted before the throne and bowed deeply. Prince Romar was his first-born, though of a native woman. His powers, though formidable, were less than a pureblood and only now beginning to manifest themselves. Anu's sharp eyes, which missed nothing, (later bards would say that he could see the falling of the sparrow) noticed that Romar's armor was dented and dulled by the fires of the battlefield, blood stained it in more than one place, but his stood tall before the throne.

It is good that such bravery be seen on one so young, Anu mused.

"You sent for me, sire?" Romar's deep voice reverberated throughout the enclosure.

Anu sat in deep thought for a few moments. Finally, in a voice so soft, his son had to strain to hear it, the Great Lord, Keeper of the Door spoke.

"You have done very well, my son. As befits a Prince of the Empire of the Eternal Flame, you have led your troops at the forefront of the Host of Angels. It is your example that our warriors have immolated. Your military genius that has resulted in the defeat of our foes time and again."

The young man allowed himself a small smile. Praise such as this from the great Anu, even to his own son was rare.

Anu motioned his son forward to perch on the edge of dais. Though brave beyond belief, Romar became uneasy; his father had never allowed anyone to sit on the dais but himself.

"My son, it is time that you be told many things, knowledge of which would have been yours in the course of time, many years in the future. But this great civil war that has torn our world apart has brought about many changes. What I will now ask of you makes it important that you learn much in a short period of time."

He paused for a long moment, clapped his hands and then glanced at the front of the pavilion. A tall armored warrior, whose build rivaled that of the Great Anu himself entered. Michael, the commander of Anu's bodyguard, bowed low.

"You called O Great One?"

Anu smiled into his beard, only Michael, the holder of the title Champion of the Gods, dared to face him so insolently. His conduct scandalized the other members of the Council of Angels. But Anu loved his warriors.

"Yes Michael, send for my Queen. Have food and drink brought for my son."

The warrior raised his right arm in salute.

"As you command, Lord," Michael, Anu's champion, turned and left.

Anu leaned back in his chair, tired beyond belief, allowing the centuries that he had lived to wash over him like a wave. He found that he was beginning to tire.

"Romar, you are my first born. You, who I had decided would one day sit on the golden throne of my fathers and rule this world. You have surpassed every expectation of your teachers and been all that a father could want. Now I have to jeopardize all of this in the best interest of my subjects."

Prince Romar was silent, waiting for his father to continue. He didn't think that he would like what he was going to hear. Anu opened his mouth to continue, but both turned as another armored figure entered the pavilion, carrying a lance and a shield, head covered by a crested silver helmet. Silently, the newcomer leaned the shield and spear against the dais, leaned forward and removed the helmet, revealing the features of a beautiful woman.

"Amazonia, my love," said the Great Anu, smiling by way of greeting.

She smiled and bowed low.

"My Lord, my son, I give you greetings on this sad day."

Anu held out his massive right hand.

"My love, come sit beside me." He said, "It is time our son knew the truth."

A pensive expression on her lovely face, Amazonia mounted the dais and gracefully sat at Anu's booted feet, leaning against the legs of the Great Lord. Romar's uneasiness increased drastically. Anu never showed affection to Queen Amazonia, even in front of his many children.

As if this was a signal, several servants entered carrying trays of food and drink. The small army of servants placed their burdens on the dais and, bowing low, backed from the presence of the Royal family. Silently the three took food and drink before settling back into their comfortable positions.

"My son," began Anu. "First, you need to know the story of your ancestry."

"I don't understand," responded Romar, a puzzled look on his handsome face.

"Romar, you know that you were born in my capital City of Ar. Your mother is the beautiful Amazonia, daughter of the King of the Santa Empire. However, what you do not know is that, while your mother is native to this planet neither I, nor the others of my race, are native."

Romar didn't know what to say; his first thought was that this was ridiculous, but the Mighty Anu was not one to joke.

"What are you saying father?" he demanded.

Anu sighed deeply, placing his massive left hand on Amazonia's muscular right shoulder, making her look dainty in comparison.

"Son, you are of supremely royal blood, descended from the first family of the first born race of the Universe, the Annunaki. When our planet Marduk became uninhabitable, our race using its scientific advances, crossed the deepness of space to look for another home where we could once again built a civilization worthy of our race. Alas, though we explored numerous planets, none were suitable. All the while, our numbers decreased as we faced the various dangers such a journey would entail. From hundreds of thousands of travelers, over the eons we traveled, our numbers were reduced to only a few thousand.

Finally, we entered this system, explored the planets that orbited the Great Sun that brings life to this world. We found two planets that could be made into suitable homes without unbelievable effort. Our planet

Eden, upon which we now live and the next planet closer to the sun, the great red planet that crosses our heavens. After the many eons of wandering among the stars we found this planet, a planet of great beauty. Resources that we sorely needed were available in great abundance here."

Anu rubbed his face with his mighty hands; perhaps even immortals feel the effects of age. Though it had been proven long ago that the body and the personality of the Annunaki could not age, perhaps some part of the emotions some part of the Id did age, thought Anu absently. With an effort, he pulled himself back to the present.

"My father, the All-knowing and All Seeing, Mighty Chronos, the eternal leader of our people decreed that we would settle on this planet and cease our nomadic wandering. A small outpost was established on the Red Planet, but the bulk of our people went into orbit around this planet. As a base of operations, my father ordered the building of a giant city in space to orbit the pole of this planet. My father and his council, called the Titans, set out to subdue the native population; millions of the natives of the planet were killed. My older brother was appointed to rule on earth while my father ruled from the Heavenly City he had built in space.

As are you, I was the military commander of Chronos' army. Mine was the duty of conquering the planet, making it safe for our people to settle and exploit the resources of this world. All of the native inhabitants except your mother's people were destroyed, no not destroyed, but massacred on orders of the Titans."

Anu paused and gazed fondly at his wife.

"Your mother was the leader of the military forces of her people. We had militarily beaten her, but rather than surrender, she gathered her forces for one last ferocious charge and succeeded in stopping our advance, allowing the women and children of her race to escape our final drive for victory. Not only did she stop our advance, but also she actually forced us to retreat, something that had never happened in the many eons that our race has conquered and traveled across the stars.

The war wound down to personal combat between she and I. We fought for hours, until one of my blows caused the chinstrap of her helmet to split and the helmet flew off of her lovely head. I was so struck by her great beauty that I refused to fight her any longer but rather overwhelmed her by sheer force, pinning her to the ground. I felt that such beauty should not die."

Amazonia laughed a delightful laugh that resounded throughout the pavilion like the tinkling of bells.

"I held you at bay for a long time, my Lord."

Anu smiled grimly through his beard.

"That you did, my love, to the point of almost getting yourself split from head to waist."

Anu reached down and filled his goblet. Slowly, he sipped the wine, allowing it to sooth the dryness of his throat. Even here in his sacred pavilion the death and destruction around them fouled the very air that filled their lungs.

"In spite of my father's orders to kill everyone, I took your mother and the remnants of her army prisoner. I thought that if I took them back, their bravery would gain a certain respect from the Titans. I thought that we could find a place for them in our empire. Unfortunately, I was naïve. I was a mighty warrior, but I was not politically experienced. I should have realized that my father could not allow even his own son to disobey his orders."

Anu paused for a long time, staring across the years, seeing in his mind's eye, his younger self, standing respectfully before his father's throne. Chronos had sat on the golden throne where Anu now sat. Asmodeus, Anu's brother, stood at Chronos' right hand. In silence, Chronos had heard his son's request that the survivors of his final campaign be spared. He listened as Anu had spoken eloquently about Amazonia's great courage and the loyalty her followers had demonstrated as they charged to certain death. Anu remembered his great shock when Chronos had screamed insanely at him about treason and unforgivable defiance. He had heard with amazement as Asmodeus had ordered him arrested for treason. Even now he felt his anger rise at the thought of his father's guards throwing themselves at him.

Finally beaten to his knees by dozens of his father's guards, he remembered being held before his father as his own father sentence him to immediate death for disobeying his orders. Anu had looked to his brother one last time for help, but Asmodeus had stood silently, a smile on his face, as Anu was drug from the royal enclosure, on his way to death.

CHAPTER TWO

Romar started at this juncture of the story. This was something he had never heard.

"Father, you have an older brother?"

Anu nodded his mighty head slowly.

'Yes, a brother and a sister."

"But, why have I never met them?" asked the surprised young man.

Anu took a deep breath. To his surprise, it was like the moment before stepping off a cliff to discuss this with his son.

"My brother and sister have never been close to me since the revolt. They blame me for many things. Some I am guilty of and some I am not." His father responded.

"Revolt?" question Romar; his world was whirling around him.

Anu growled in frustration, this was not going well, he thought.

At that moment the lovely Amazonia placed a dainty hand on his knee.

"My Lord, let me tell our son." She said softly.

With a grunt, Anu leaned back in his throne, closing his eyes as he pictured the events of so many years ago. With all his power, he was helpless to change what had been, what he now knew would be.

Amazonia leaned forward, taking her son's right hand between her own battle roughened palms.

"Romar, your own father was taken out at the orders of his own father to be killed. I saw what happened, because my few remaining warriors and I were already being held at the place of execution, waiting to die. Without my Lord's knowledge, his rightful war captives had been taken by the royal guards and, without trial taken to a place of execution. Chronos intended that none of us were to see another sunrise.

Chronos had sent your father's own brother to oversee the execution of his younger son. This meant nothing to us, but then we saw Anu, our rightful conqueror, beaten, bloodied and being drug across the field to that bloody place of execution by a mob of Royal Guards. We couldn't understand why our conqueror was being brought out to join those of us who were to be executed."

"But why?" demanded Romar, incensed at the unfairness of what had happened. "His own father wanted his son executed like common criminal."

"Because he disobeyed his father's orders to destroy all of my people," answered Amazonia patiently.

Romar stared for a long moment at his parents.

"But why would that be reason to kill him?"

Anu interrupted at this point.

"To disobey the words of the Supreme God brings death" his voice heavy and leaden.

Romar sat quietly and considered the words of both his father and his mother. He felt his world slipping away.

"And then what happened?" finally asked the Prince.

Amazonia glanced quickly at Anu and, seeing he intended to say nothing, cleared her throat to continue.

"The firing squad had encircled us, and was aiming their photon blasters at us. Asmodeus---"

Romar raised his hand for silence.

"Photon blaster? Asmodeus?" he questioned, "I don't understand."

It was Amazonia's turn to sigh and glance again at her Lord.

"My son, we use the weapons of war that we have now due to the banning of much more powerful weapons that your father felt should not be used against humans. My Lord Anu has at his disposal weapons of unbelievable power. As for Asmodeus-----"

"Asmodeus?" exploded Romar, "What has the Evil One to do with this?"

Amazonia bit her lip for a moment, she hadn't meant to name their great enemy, but now the cat was out of the bag.

"My son," interrupted Anu, as he leaned forward to fix his stern gaze on his son, "Asmodeus is my brother. He is an Annunaki of God rank, even as I."

Romar opened his mouth to speak, but Anu stopped him with a gesture.

"You interrupt your mother."

Romar took a deep breath and bowed from his seated position.

"My apologies mother, please continue."

Amazonia flipped her long hair from her face.

"Asmodeus raised his sword to signal his soldier to fire when a mighty force came broiling across the plain to the rescue. Your father's second in command, Michael, had learned what had transpired in the throne room and taken matters into his own hands. The Army loved your father but had little use for Asmodeus. For some time, it had been clear that Chronos had become just a puppet for his son, Asmodeus. Your father had always been known for being his own man. When the choice came down to backing one or the other of them Anu won. In short, the Army revolted."

Anu stirred on his golden throne and glanced toward the entrance of the pavilion, daylight was waning. Already flickering torchlight was visible through the entrance.

"Time grows short my wife," commented Anu.

"Asmodeus' followers managed to buy time enough for the coward to run from the field and take shelter in the great palace. Chronos called out his bodyguard and ordered them to move to challenge my Lord under the command of the Lady Athena, sister to Asmodeus. Though well-schooled in the arts of war, she and her forces were no match for the Army under your father's command. Her forces were decimated and, as her right as a goddess, she was given the choice of surrender or personal combat with Anu. She chose combat and was vanquished."

"Killed?" questioned Romar.

Amazonia shook her head and held up one hand.

"All will be revealed my son," she replied by way of answer.

"Anu, at the head of his loyal forces that had followed him through numerous campaigns against my people, stormed the Royal Palace. Chronos and Asmodeus were barricaded in the great hall with their most fanatical followers and creatures of unbelievable horror."

"Let me, wife," interrupted the mighty Anu.

Obediently, Amazonia fell silent, waiting her lord to speak.

Anu ran one mighty hand across his face as if to block out sights he would rather not see.

"I had known that Asmodeus aspired to rule this world. Frankly, as firstborn of Chronos, and Crown Prince, I thought it was his right to rule. I said nothing when Chronos appointed Asmodeus as Prince of the World. I was content to be commander of the Army. Unfortunately, for us all, Asmodeus aspired to more than simply the rule of a single planet.

Without the knowledge of Chronos, Asmodeus had contacted our greatest enemies, the Draconian, and made a pact. We had warred with them in the early days of the creation of the universe and banished them to another dimension. We had long ago developed the technology to use the other dimensions as prisons, but we were as children when it came to knowledge of what aftereffects this would have. Energies that they were exposed to in that dimension had changed them into true monsters, and increased their powers beyond all comprehension.

They came into our dimension once again without our knowledge as Asmodeus, through some of his many agents, had ensured that for a short window of time, our dimensional security systems were off line. Even more reprehensible, Asmodeus had used his authority as Royal Prince to gain access to knowledge that had been forbidden by Chronos, himself. Using what he learned, Asmodeus had become a mighty sorcerer in his own right, and then increased that power when he had found allies among our people who gave him use of their own powers.

Once here in our dimension, the Draconians used their own powers to assist Asmodeus in opening a permanent portal to our plane from their own."

Anu paused to pour himself another goblet of wine and took a sip.

"When we burst into the throne room, Chronos was near death, lying in a crumpled heap at the foot of the dais. You don't know it yet, but it takes massive force to kill a full-blooded Annunaki. Asmodeus had ascended the golden throne and was surrounded by the Draconian wizards he had summoned to aid him. For a long moment, the two forces gauged each other, no one wanting to be the first to fire. Then, tiring of the standoff, I gave the signal to advance."

Anu rose and stepped from the dais. He paced a long track in front of his family.

"The air was filled with the screams of dying men, the sizzle of energy weapons and the clang of swords. The carnage was horrible. Some of the best and brightest of our race died on the floor of the throne room, unable to resist the terrible weapons of the Draconians."

He paused and looked across the years to that day.

"Was it worth it?" fretted the Great Lord.

"Lord, how can you say that?" gasped Amazonia. "You brought peace and prosperity to millions. You saved us all from the followers of the Evil One. You made this planet into a paradise."

"But at what cost?" said Anu, his mighty head bent as he studied the floor before him. "How many died so that I could rule our empire?"

As his wife began to regain her feet to remonstrate with him, he raised one massive arm.

"No, wife, what's done it done, but I may still have regrets."

Any straightened and faced his son.

"It seemed like days, but it was only hours when I, your mother and Michael stood at the front of the gold throne, our forces arrayed behind us. Asmodeus sat regally on the stolen throne, his Draconian allies fled back through their doorway, his Annunaki and human followers decimated."

Amazonia helped herself to a grape from the platter before her and took up the story.

"Asmodeus sat on his stolen throne as if he were the victor and not the vanquished.

"What do you want, brother?" he had asked in disdain.

"You father had said nothing, but grabbed Asmodeus by the front of his robe and tossed him across the floor like so much rubbish. The Evil One had struggled to his feet and roared his defiance as he rushed at my Lord, a hidden dagger in one upraised fist. Michael had moved to protect your father, but brushing him aside, my Lord had blocked the blow and rendered Asmodeus unconscious with a might fist. "

With a deep sign, Anu stopped pacing in front of his son.

"Romar," he said, "I made a great error that day. I had conquered an empire, but wanted to avoid further bloodshed. Rather than executing them, I banished Asmodeus and Athena to their home cities. I stripped them of their armies and their weapons. I thought that this would end the problems, but there was more bloodshed when the Titans, who still controlled the Heavenly City, refused to submit to my rule and many of Asmodeus' followers resided in the Martian City. There were troubles for the next hundred years, but finally after one set back after another for the followers of Chronos, the Titans submitted, we bombed the Martian City and I was declared to uncontested ruler of the Annunaki Empire."

"I had fought back to save my life. I murdered and destroyed to become uncontested ruler of the mightiest empire that has ever existed. But of all the bodies I walked across in my rise to the throne, the two that that I should have killed I did not. When I should have hardened my heart and been my strongest, I lost my resolve. My squeamishness in not executing my siblings has led to this civil war and all of this death and destruction."

Amazonia moved to come to him to comfort him, but Anu stayed her with a look.

Romar stood and faced his father.

"But that is history father, what does it have to do with today?"

Anu smiled grimly, his radiant eyes boring deep into those of his son.

"When this war is over, my son, I, your mother, and the majority of our people, are withdrawing from this planet to the Heavenly City."

Romar stood in deep thought for a long moment.

"And I father?"

"Every prison needs a guard, my son."

CHAPTER THREE

In the golden throne room of the royal palace in Etrea, Asmodeus paced the floor in anger. His sister, Athena sat on a smaller copy of the great golden throne that surmounted the raised dais that dominated the room, itself an exact copy of Anu's massive throne. On their knees in the center for the room were three men in full battle dress, their helmets cradled under their right arms, armor blackened and dented.

"Lord, their forces are unstoppable. We have been forced back against the walls of the city itself. Defeat is inevitable," spoke the senior of the three.

Asmodeus stopped his pacing and glared at his military commanders.

"Defeat is unthinkable. You are obviously bunglers, unable to handle your duties," roared the massive figure before them.

Enraged, the senior of the three jumped to his feet, his anger outweighing his awe at his ruler.

"I have been undefeated in over a hundred battles. I, and my father before me, have carried your standard to the farthest reaches of the world. Using our proven battle tactics, we have handed your enemy one defeat after another. It was your sending us into battle on the whims of that whore that sits beside you is what brought us to this ruin," he snapped.

"You dare!" roared Asmodeus.

"How dare you!" spat Athena, as spittle flew form her perfect lips.

"You have left me no choice, but to leave your service!" shot back the Officer, spinning on his heel to leave the throne room.

"You leave only when I release you!" yelled Asmodeus, stretching forth his right arm. An arrow of flame flew from his fingertips and engulfed the angry soldier. His hideous screams echoed throughout the palace as he crumpled to his knees. It was a burned ruin that collapsed to the marble floor.

Asmodeus staggered slightly and made his way to his throne. He turned his eyes, drained and empty, toward the two terrified soldiers that still crouched in terror before his throne.

"Milo Enturde."

"Yes Lord." whimpered the older of the two.

"Is it true that we are defeated?" he asked quietly.

"Y—Yes, my Lord, the battle is lost," quaked the soldier, expecting certain death.

Asmodeus glanced over at the lady Athena, who sat primly on her own lesser throne.

"It is time, sister," he said softly.

Athena turned her lovely head and looked at an attendant standing like a statue against the wall.

"Send for my son."

The silent attendant bowed, they all had had their tongues removed at birth, on order of the Lady Athena and left the room. In a few moments, the attendant returned and resumed his place against the wall. The tall figure that had followed the attendant crossed the floor to stop before the thrones.

"My Lord, mother," he said with a deep bow.

The Lady Athena smiled at the sight of her tall handsome son. Rather than dressed in battle garb he was dressed all in black, his figure obscured by a long cape that barely touched the floor.

"Dakkar, my son: how are things with you?" asked his mother in a soft voice.

"All is well, mother," he said in a sardonic tone, 'and with you?"

"How are our friends?" interrupted the Lord Asmodeus.

"Impatient, Lord," responded Dakkar.

"Well, they need be impatient no longer. Release them against our enemies," ordered Asmodeus.

"Even the living dead?" asked Dakkar in anticipation.

"Even so," ordered Asmodeus.

Dakkar bowed low before his Lord.

"You do realize there will be no stopping them. They will kill everything in their path."

Asmodeus snorted his impatience.

"So! They are weak, they follow my brother. They should die."

"As you wish, Lord, so shall it be," said Dakkar as he bowed his way from the throne room.

CHAPTER FOUR

And so it was when the Hosts of the Lord stormed the gates of the city, they were met first with the force of human arms, but when the bulk of the defenders had been dispatched, they attackers met with a horde seemed to have come straight out of a nightmare. Every type of monster and evil being anyone ever heard of came swarming out of the lower regions of the Royal Palace. These creatures fell upon everything in their path, whether defender or invader. They were unstoppable.

Now it was the turn of the Host of the Lord Anu to be forced to fall back before the animalistic fury of the creatures. Romar paused in his battle as he felt eyes boring into him. He glanced around and saw the figure of Asmodeus on the walls of the city, laughing insanely at the death and destruction before him. At his side was a tall, slim man dressed in black, it was his eyes that Romar had felt. Somehow, he knew that this was someone he would one day have to face directly.

PART ONE

MURDER IN ACADEMIA

CHAPTER FIVE

Professor Amos Bennett was almost trembling with excitement as he rushed past his receptionist, a plainly wrapped package clutched tightly under his left arm and his dark leather briefcase clutched under his right. He was a somewhat comical figure as he raced down the wide hall of the History Building, dodging surprised students like a broken field football player. To the relief of the students had hadn't yet run into in his visible excitement, he reached his office door and almost tore it from its hinges as he literally dove into the office.

Addie Kincade, for the last twenty-five years his mother cum receptionist, glanced up with surprise as the Professor dashed madly across her office carrying a package like a football. His suit was rumpled and his unstylishly long fine hair was standing at attention. He ran into his office, slammed the door, then jerked it back open and paused in the doorway to his private office.

"Addie, call Amanda and tell her to come immediately and see if you can get in contact with Sheila."

He paused a moment and then shook his head.

"No!" He almost danced in his excitement. "No, forget calling Sheila; get me a reservation on the first plane to Albuquerque. I'll go to her."

Before Addie could say a word in response, the Professor slammed the door again, this time she heard the lock click. Smiling, she slowly shook her head; the Professor was always coming up with something of earth shaking importance. In a few weeks, he would be onto some other project, the classic example of the absent-minded professor. He was like a little boy, but she loved him dearly. With a sigh, she reached for the phone and began to dial.

In his office, Professor Bennett carefully, placed his package in the center of his cluttered desk and reached over to close the blinds. That detail attended to, Professor Bennett approached his desk, so excited that his hands were shaking. Dropping into his battered leather desk chair, he switched on the desk lamp and slowly, reverently pulled the package closer to him. For a long moment, he just held it and felt the joy of possession sweep through him.

"I can't believe it!" he whispered, "I can't believe I finally got it!"

With trembling fingers, he began to unfasten the wrapping that held his treasure. Finally, giving into impatience, he ripped the paper from the object; tossing the paper carelessly aside, Dr. Bennett held his prize underneath the light from the desk lamp. In all its' glory, the little statue gleamed as if made of pure gold. The figure was a reproduction of one of the major gods of ancient Sumeria, the cradle of modern civilization. To the average individual, the figure was ugly, but to Dr. Bennett, it was the most beautiful thing in the world.

"Beautiful, simply beautiful," breathed Bennett handling the statue as if it was a precious gem.

It had long been Professor Bennett's belief that there had existed a very advanced civilization prior to the glory of ancient Sumeria. He had theorized that this ancient, unknown people had given the earliest known civilizations their gods and their religious beliefs. Being independently wealthy, having inherited a great deal of money and property from his parents, Professor Bennett had traveled the world looking for the smallest scrap of evidence to support his theory.

In his hands, was the proof that he had sought across the world and sacrificed so much to find. Much of his inheritance and an irreplaceable part of his life had gone into the search. In his enthusiasm, Professor Bennett had uprooted his family and headed into the jungles of South America then continued his search in the deserts of the Middle East. He had taken his delicate young wife and his two young daughters into some of the most primitive areas on the planet. He had dragged them from country to country, digging, poking and prying into the secrets of the past.

In fact, he had been so concerned with the past that he had actually neglected the present, not noticing when his wife began to wither and die in the inhospitable climates in which they spent most of their time.

The death of Sarah Bennett, his beautiful young wife, in Iran some twenty years before, had shattered the idealistic young professor. Suddenly, he was bereft of his closest friend and left with two infant daughters, with no one to care for them except himself. At loose ends, the grieving father, and husband, gathered his children for one last trip, back to the United States, back to the busy, bustling New York City that he had wanted so much to leave.

Based on his published research and his status in the field of ancient civilizations, New York University quickly offered Amos a full professorship. Prior to the tragic death of his wife, Bennett had turned down several such offers, looking at a teaching position as a living death, but now he grabbed the offered position eagerly. Reining in his natural wanderlust, Amos Bennett settled in to create a stable home life for his two daughters.

With a shake of his head, Amos Bennett brought himself back to the present. In his hands was what he had searched the world to find, proof that a highly technical civilization had flourished in the Middle East almost a half a million years ago. Made of a totally unknown metal alloy, the figurine of the creature, worshipped as a god by the ancient Sumerians, represented a level of technology unknown in ancient times.

Finally, putting the statue back on his desk, Professor Bennett, opened the upper right hand drawer of his desk and rummaged among its contents until he found the small tape recorder he sought. Pressing the record and play switches, Professor Bennett leaned back in his chair and began to speak, never taking his eyes off the figure before him.

"Today is the 24th of October. I am dictating this in my office at the University. I just returned from a meeting with Arnold Steiner, of Mansfield's Auction House. He showed me two items; one is a statute or figurine approximately eighteen inches high made of an unknown alloy. The statue is of a minor Sumerian god, or at least the Sumerians worshipped this entity as one of their gods of evil.

Based on my research, I have come to the belief that this entity represented by the statue was a living creature that somehow had such an effect on the Sumerians that he became an integral part of their religious pantheon. However, I am getting ahead of myself."

Snapping off the recorder and placing it on the desk, Professor Bennett again took the statue in his hands and caressed it like a man would a woman. His eyes closed and his breath deepened as he lost himself in the sensations coming from the idol. Finally, with a shuttering, deep breath, the Professor forced himself to put the statue back on the desk and take up the recorder.

"Along with the statue, Steiner gave me a very old copy of an even older manuscript. The language used in the manuscript is ancient Aramaic. It is my belief that the original document from which this copy of taken was actually written by the proto civilization that I have long believed flourished around the world.

"Even more amazingly, the manuscript given me by Steiner supports my theories of unknown advanced civilizations before our own. According to the manuscript, there was a race of mentally advanced people that lived along the Algerian coast approximately 10,000 years ago. Confirming the text, evidence of such a race having existed along the Algerian coast has only recently been found by archeologists, which would, in my mind, also tend to confirm the rest of the literally unbelievable information contained in the manuscript.

"I might make note that orthodox history is completely silent regarding the Mullion Culture, as researchers have named this recently discovered culture. What is known is that the skeletons that have been found from this race show that their cranial capacity is in excess of 2,000 cc., much greater than our own 1400 cc. capacity. Based on cranial capacity, it is quite possible that this race was our intellectual superiors.

"According to the information available to me through this remarkable text, the Mullions, who actually called themselves the Annunaki, were the descendants of an even older race, which inhabited Europe, Africa and Asia some five hundred centuries ago. According to the detailed information in the text, in its declined the race of the Annunaki had formed a Kingdom which they called AR, which was a rich flourishing country, stretching from the Algerian coast, east almost to modern day Moscow, and north to the north sea.

"It is interesting to note that 10,000 to 12,000 years ago would place the height of the late Annunaki people or the Mullion people, as they are currently referred to at about the probable time of the end of fabled Atlantis. There is perhaps some possible connection between this race and the fabled Atlanteans, which would deserve further investigation."

He clicked off the recorder for a moment, taping it gently against his chin. Swiveling his chair around he raised his eyes toward the ceiling for a long time. Finally, he turned the recorder back on and began to speak.

"The manuscript reports that the decline of the Annunaki or Mullion civilization came as a result of the invasion of a sect of assassins that worshipped a leader, ruler or god called Asmodeus, the evil one. The text states that Asmodeus demanded the sacrifice of the first born of the rulers of the Annunaki be made to his service and enforced his demands with his legion of followers and also by opening the gates that separated this world from the netherworld and releasing a creature or creatures called the Piasa.

"Faced with enslavement, the text states that the Annunaki released the demons of their forefathers in one last great battle with Asmodeus and his legion of followers. The mighty war that followed ravaged the known world and reduced the mighty Annunaki civilization to a mere shell of its former glory. From a population of several million, the text reports that only a few hundred thousand of the Annunaki were left after the Great War."

Professor Bennett stopped talking for a few minutes, turning to a nearby bookcase. After pulling several books from the bookcases that covered two of the walls from floor to ceiling and flipping to the index, he finally found the book he wanted and returned to his chair. Opening it to the page he wanted, Professor Bennett picked up the recorder and began to speak.

"As a partial confirmation of the details of the Aramaic text furnished me by Steiner, I offer a report written by Father Marquette, the well-known Jesuit explorer who explored the Mississippi in the mid-1600s. In his published journal in 1681, he wrote about rock paintings that he saw painted high on cliffs along the Mississippi. The creatures so pictured resembled our beliefs in how the prehistoric Pterodactyl would have appeared in life. The Indians referred to the creatures so pictured as the Piasa."

He paused for a minute and flipped a few pages in his book. Marking the spot with his finger, he turned the recorder back on.

"I would also point to the writing of Professor John Russell who wrote of the Piasa in the July, 1848 issue of "The Evangelical Magazine and Gospel Advocate", he writes that, during an expedition to remote section of the Matto Grasso in South America, accompanied by an Indian guide, he entered the a remote cave which legend reported had been the dwelling of one of the mysterious Piasa. He reported that a tunnel in the rear of the cave led to a tremendous cavern. The floor of the giant cavern was literally carpeted with the bones of thousands of humans, men, women and children, all alleged to have been killed and eaten by the dreaded Piasa. I would view this an independent confirmation of the information in the text."

Professor Bennett stopped and flipped a few more pages.

"Returning to the information from the text," he began, "it is reported that though Asmodeus lost the war with the Annunaki, Asmodeus proved rather more difficult to kill. The text refers to great battles that destroyed continents and changed the face of the land, so the energies and weapons unleashed by both sides must have been of tremendous power. If accurate, this war would explain why archeologists have never found any recognizable technological remains of the proto civilization. This is where the legends end.

"Now we go from legend to the manuscript I recently obtained. According to what I have read so far, having defeated their enemy, the mighty Asmodeus, the wise men of the Annunaki decided that the wisest thing to do was to imprison their captive as far away from their homes as possible. According to the text, Asmodeus was imprisoned in a block of some type of material that acted as a damper on his tremendous powers. Once imprisoned, the block containing the god of evil was imprisoned in a great cavern across the endless sea from the remains of the Kingdom of Ar and out of reach of his surviving followers.

"The location of the prison and the secret for freeing the evil one were etched into a small golden disk that was kept in the great temple of the all father god, the Great Anu. The instructions in the text make it clear that the statue, which I have in my possession and the disk, which sounds suspiciously like the one that I obtained from Steiner several years ago and gave to Sheila as a gift, are both necessary in order to free Asmodeus from his eternal.

"According to the text, the god Asmodeus was actually the brother of the Great Anu and thus also immortal. Anu felt that there was a constant danger that Asmodeus would one day escape from his cavern prison and would be a constant threat to the peoples of this world for all time. To help his people, the Great Anu is supposed to have sent his son down from his heavenly palace to protect the peoples of Earth. His son, also being immortal is alleged to walk the earth for all time."

A stabbing pain in his head caused Professor Bennett to lean back and close his eyes as he rubbed his brow.

"As closely as I have been able to decipher the text," he continued, "the son of the Great Anu would correspond to the mythical Hercules, son of the mythical Zeus, of ancient European tradition. Supposedly this Hercules fellow is charged to walk the planet forever making sure that Asmodeus and his follows aren't up to anything.

"However, as a great philosopher once said, all things must balance. Asmodeus, anticipating the need for an immortal assistant on the outside, so to speak, prior to his defeat, fed one of his most trusted followers the "food of the gods". This food is supposed to have made his follower immortal, with the same powers as the gods of the Heavens."

Suddenly Professor Bennett shivered as the temperature in the room dropped to just above freezing, he could see his breath in the air.

Dropping the recorder into the partially opened drawer, he staggered to his feet and raised the window blinds to the sunlight. He reached for the window latch and froze, his mouth hanging open in disbelief. Literally hovering outside his office window, four floors above the street, standing on nothing but air, was a man, wearing a scarlet robe, which billowed out behind him.

"Bennett, I have come for you," intoned the figure in a spectral voice. "You have something which is not yours."

Shaken from his paralyzing fear, Bennett dropped the blinds back down and darted to his desk. The figure was swept up and placed carefully into the credenza under the window; the briefcase was shoved out of sight beneath the desk. Ripping open the bottom right hand drawer, Bennett shoved aside old papers and finally raised his hand, his Webley-Scott revolver clutched in his right hand. He spun at a sound behind him.

"I have come for you, Bennett," stated the figure that had been hovering in the air outside his window; now standing less than four feet behind him.

Amos Bennett held the revolver against his leg and backed away.

"Who are you?" he demanded, his voice shaking.

"I am known as the Master, leader of the Legions of Asmodeus, the eternal god of evil. I have come for the statute that you received from the one called Steiner," he said, moving slowly toward Bennett, cutting him off from the door.

"W-W-Who?" asked Bennett moving to his left, which unfortunately placed him further from the door.

The Master smiled a slow sinister smile, as he continued to maneuver the older Professor into a corner.

"Let's not be tiresome, Professor Bennett, Mr. Steiner told me all about your recent acquisitions before his most untimely death. You recently received a statute of Asmodeus from him as well as a worthless manuscript. More importantly, some time ago, you also received the Seal of the Great Anu, may he burn in the ire of hell, the second key, if you will, to the prison holding my Master. I have come for them."

Bennett's mind reeled, Steiner dead, it seemed impossible, he had just left him, but a man able to hover four floors above the street was also impossible.

"Why do you want these things, assuming that I do have them?" demanded the frightened Professor, his mind searching for some way to summon help.

The sinister figure smiled again and moved a step closer.

"Quite simple, human, I intend to free Asmodeus so that he can rule this world as he was meant to do. This world was meant to be the home of the gods, not a puny race such as yours."

Bennett was staggered as he anticipated the devastation that would be visited on the human race.

"But you are human yourself. Surely you have some feeling left for your own race," he charged, clutching the revolver even tighter.

The Master considered Bennett with something close to respect.

"So you have learned something in your years of fruitless searching. Perhaps I was once raised as a human, but I was not born of human parents. My Master placed me with a human family to learn how to pass as a human. The truth is that my Master made me even as he, a God."

"You were Asmodeus' follower that was fed the Food of the Gods!" gasped Bennett.

"You are very perceptive, old man. Too bad you have to die. You know too much."

Finally, Bennett felt the bookcase pressing against his back; he knew that he had nowhere to go.

"Even a god can die!" Bennett yelled as he swung up the pistol and pulled the trigger.

CHAPTER SIX

Addie Kincade hung up the phone and returned to her typing. She was watching the clock, anticipating the arrival of five o'clock and quitting time. Having long entertained a crush on the eccentric Professor Bennett, she had finally decided to ask him out to dinner, since it was obvious that he was not going to ask her. At times, she felt that Bennett looked at her like he did the furniture, in the room, but beneath his notice.

The afternoon passed uneventfully, she worked her way through the mountain of paperwork that routinely crossed her desk. There were numerous groups that wanted Professor Bennett to submit articles or make speeches regarding his research. He seldom had the time, and tended to ignore the requests. It fell to Addie to send the proper responses and keep his schedule under some type of control. She was his secretary, his assistant and his mother. Without her, Professor Bennett would be hopelessly bogged down in the administrative details of his job.

She got up from her desk, a pile of letters to be signed by the Professor and telephone message to be returned clutched in her hand, and started for his office door. As she reached for the knob, the corridor door opened and Professor Arthur Peters, the Department head entered.

"Addie, my dear, is your boss man in his inner sanctum?

Addie Kincade smiled at the dashing young Adrkministrator, who though he had long been one of her favorites, was always, number two behind her Professor.

"As usual with a new prize from that auction house."

At that moment, the sound of several gunshots came from

Professor Bennett's office. Crossing the office in two strides, Professor Peters grabbed the doorknob and twisted, the knob didn't move. Now the sounds of a titanic struggle could be heard from the inner office.

With a grunt, Peters through his two hundred plus pounds against the door and the lock gave way. Peters and Addie Kincade both stopped in shock as they saw the shambles that had been Professor Bennett's cluttered office. Professor Bennett himself lay crumpled against the far wall as a man in a scarlet cloak towered above him.

Peters immediately rushed forward, but the stranger grabbed the former all state wrestler in one hand and tossed him effortlessly across the office to crash against the wall. Addie Kincade grabbed the closest weapon to protect her Professor, which happened to be a heavy ancient Templar cross that normally hung on the wall behind the Professor's chair. Holding the cross by its' base, she swung the makeshift weapon with all her might just as the stranger sensed her movement and turned toward her. The upper portion of the cross caught him on the side of the head and knocked him from his feet.

Staggered, the stranger rushed toward the windows, pausing to grab a small statue from the floor where it had fallen from the overturned credenza. He straightened with a roar of triumph, which turned into a shriek of pain as Addie slammed the heavy Templar Cross across his broad back, knocking him to his knees. Clutching the statue under one arm, the injured man sprang forward and crashed through the locked window, carrying the sash with him.

Dropping the cross to thud on the carpet, Addie hurried over to Professor Bennett, cradling his bleeding head in her arms as she whispered low endearments in his ears. She was still holding her Professor when Professor Peters came to her side and gently took Bennett's wrist and felt for a pulse. With a deep sigh, he gently placed the limp arm across his colleague's chest.

"Addie, I'm afraid he's dead."

PART TWO

THE CAPTIVE

CHAPTER SEVEN

There was nothing but desolation and endless sand as far as the eye could see. Interstate 25 was a wide, long, hot surface; shimmers of heat waves could be seen coming from the hardstand. To make matters worse, the clouds, which had hung low all day, were now menacing in their darkness. Even the most inexperienced tenderfoot could tell that a heavy-duty storm was brewing. Unfortunately the individual driving along the highway had never been to New Mexico before.

Amanda Bennett pulled her rental car off to the side of the road and consulted the map one more time. She was certain that the turn off she was to take was somewhere in the area, but for the life of her, she could not find it. She threw the map to the floor in disgust and, checking her mirror, pulled back onto the road. In her anger and frustration, she didn't notice the black car following some distance behind her.

"What has that sister of mine gotten herself into now?" She muttered to herself. "Why would that hair brained girl come to the backside of nowhere?

Her thoughts went back to the letter that had arrived at her office only a few days ago. As executrix of her father's estate, Amanda had spent a small fortune discovering her sister's whereabouts so that she could be sent her share of the inheritance, which was a considerable sum of money. Leave it to Sheila to turn a simple business matter into a major problem.

Under their father's will, the bulk of the funds were in an account that required that they both be present to sign the necessary papers for the release of the funds.

Sheila, as usual had no concept of business, her one and only response was a letter that said that she was not up to coming to the big city at this time. Sheila was lonesome, her current flame having run off with another. Sheila was now staying with some teacher in a small town called El Noche, New Mexico. As usual, Amanda was being forced to come to get her little sister.

Amanda Bennett was a successful businesswoman, having clawed herself to the top of the brokerage world in New York. She saw herself as a dynamic forceful businesswoman. Most of her friends saw her as a prim, vindictive, spiteful bitch, not above using her body to get an advantage. But even her greatest critics had to admit that she was one hell of a beautiful woman.

Amanda was thirty-one, tall, about 5'9" in her stocking feet, flashing dark blue eyes, with long, thick, ebony hair that glimmered in even the faintest light. Full figured, she had long showgirl's legs and a chest that could rival that of the most glamorous centerfold. These gifts, she had used to work her way to the top of her chosen profession. More than one man had fallen victim to her charms, only to find himself thrown by the wayside when a better man came along.

Amanda was a hard eyed, iron willed harpy, whose only real weakness was that she cared for her only sister, Sheila. Sheila was her mirror image, with crimson locks and bright, sparkling green eyes in place of Amanda's darker coloring. Sheila, who though every bit as beautiful and bright as Amanda, lacked only Amanda's driving ambition, for Sheila cared for those she interacted with, rather than used them. Sheila who even now, thought Amanda, was at the mercy of those dirty cowboy types in some pigsty of a wide spot in the road called El Noche, New Mexico.

"Probably that same type of white trash as at that gas station," she snapped, talking to herself in the rearview mirror. She was still seething at what had happened to her.

Amanda had flown into the Albuquerque Airport and rented a car for the long drive to El Noche. She had stopped at the Texaco station in Socorro, New Mexico to ask directions. In her fashionably short skirt, which showed her long legs to their best advantage, Amanda had attracted a lot of attention. Several of the older men who were sitting around the station had even made crude suggestions, laughing uproariously when she had shown her annoyance. Secretly, Amanda hated men, but she had to work with them daily. She didn't have to put up with crude remarks, however.

For a moment, Amanda had a mental picture of her beautiful sister, Sheila lying nude, on her back, on a stained table, her long crimson hair hanging down toward the floor. Crowded around her were dozens of ugly smelly men in dirty jeans, who ran their equally dirty hands running all over her sister's pristine body.

"If it's the last thing that I ever do, I'll take you away from this wretched sand pile and back to New York where you belong!" swore Amanda, gripping the wheel even tighter as a sudden gust of wind caused her car to swerve.

In spite of herself, Amanda had to have a twinge of worry regarding the weather. The dark clouds were coming lower, the afternoon was getting darker, and she switched on her headlights. The wind was blowing in stronger gusts, causing her to seriously worry about being forced off the road. Sheets of rain began to meet her on the long dark, empty highway. Nowhere could she see any sign of humanity. For a big city girl, such vast distances were unthinkable and intimidated. For the first time in her life, Amanda Bennett was not in control of the situation and she was scared.

Suddenly, Amanda slammed on the brakes, her car fishtailing on the wet pavement. In the glow of her headlights, she saw the final indignity in a long line of indignities, a detour sign. The Interstate was closed, it seemed. Frantically, she looked for a way to turn around and noticed that another sign pointed to the no name exit immediately to her left. Easing off the brake, she slowly drove up the off ramp, straining to see any road signs through the driving rain and stopped at the stop sign.

Amanda was concentrating so intently on looking for direction signs that she failed to notice the dark figure that had waited emotionless in the ditch behind the detour sign. She didn't notice him use a cupped flashlight to signal the black car that had followed her for so many miles. She didn't see the car cut its lights and follow her up the exit, nor did she see the figure on the road drag the detour sign onto the side of the road and topple it into the ditch. Amanda Bennett saw nothing except the distant lights of the small restaurant to her right, a mile down the side road.

With a feeling of relief, Amanda drove slowly through the driving rain and pulled into the parking lot of the restaurant. Only a few cars were in the gravel parking lot, so she pulled her car as close to the front entrance as possible. The car that had been following her pulled to a stop just off the road and sat idling until Amanda dashed from her car to the door of the restaurant. With a jerk, she pulled the door open and almost jumped inside. As if to help, the rain became even harder, making it almost impossible to see more than a few feet.

At this point the black car pulled slowly across the gravel to stop but a few feet from Amanda's car. Under the cover of the rolling thunder and crashing lightning, the passenger door of the black car swung open and a slight figure exited to stand for a moment in the driving rain. With a few steps, the figure was crouched beside the rental car, slipping a flat metal bar into the top of the door, just above the lock. With a few quick movements of the bar, the figure pulled the door open and slipped into the back seat, and slid from view. The black car pulled away and drove slowly to the end of the parking lot, swinging around so that it faced the rental car. The engine shut off, all was silent except for the crashing of the storm.

The restaurant was almost completely deserted. Only the hostess had been in evidence when Amanda had entered the building, an odd woman, plain, and very submissive. She never said a word, merely leading

Amanda into the restaurant area. Efficiently, Amanda Bennett was quickly seated at a table near a large roaring fire, nursing a cup of hot chocolate. She was soaked through and through, she was sure that her expensive dress was ruined. She knew that her carefully arranged hair was certainly a sight. Her very expensive, leather spike heeled shoes were certainly water logged.

"That girl's going to pay me for all of this!" She muttered to herself, as she shivered in her damp clothes. "If there wasn't so much money at stake, I'd let her stay in this God forsaken desert."

In spite of her anger, Amanda had to admit that the restaurant was a soothing place, with its' Southwestern decor and tastefully decorated dining room. From the red tile floor to the aged beams, which held up the ceiling, it was a classic example of southwest architecture. In the spreading warmth of the cheerful room, Amanda was beginning to relax as her dress began to slowly dry from both her body heat and the fire.

"Sumtin else for you, Senorita?" asked a respectful voice behind her.

Amanda started and swung around to see that it was an elderly Hispanic waiter standing slightly to her rear.

"What, oh, nothing, thanks. This is fine." she relied, shivering again, and pulling her chair closer to the fire.

Amanda realized that as soaked as her dress was, that silhouetted against the fire, her thin fashionable dress could be seen through, but she was so cold, she didn't care. Besides, the old Mexican waiter seemed harmless enough.

"Wait," she said as he began to turn away, "there is something you can do for me."

"Yes, Senorita? Servador de usted," he replied respectfully.

"Are you familiar with this area?"

"Si, Senorita, I have lived here all my life. I have always been here." He replied with a shy smile.

"I have to meet someone, uh, a relative, somewhere near here. I think I'm lost. Do you know where the town of El Noche might be located?" she asked, sipping her drink.

"El Noche?" Questioned the old man, "Why does the Senorita wish to know where might be El Noche? There are few people in El Noche."

Something unusual in his voice caused Amanda to look up at him curiously.

"I'm to meet my sister there." she said, "But it doesn't show on my map. Do you know how to get there?"

The old Mexican clasped his hands tightly together.

"El Noche is a very old place, no one goes there anymore. The Senorita would do well to stay away from that place. It is cursed by the evil one. It has always been an evil place. Don't go, Senorita, you will die!" He stammered, slowly backing away from her as he hurriedly crossed himself.

Amanda finished her drink, reached in her purse and threw a couple of dollars on the table. Superstitious poppycock, the evil one, indeed, she thought, as she rose to her feet.

"I don't know anything about this evil one or really care about local superstition. Do you know where it is?" she asked again, a bit more emphatically.

"Si, Senorita. Yo sabe, but please, do not go there." he repeated, "I beg you. It is the home of the ancient evil one."

"Old man, if you know where the damn place is, please tell me!" She finally demanded, her ready temper flaming at his stalling. The old waiter merely shrugged and mumbled something unintelligible.

"Perhaps I may be of service, my dear?" asked a deep voice from behind her.

Amanda spun around so fast that she almost lost her balance, one heel of her ruined shoes twisting under her weight. Only a strong hand under her elbow kept her from falling to the carpeted floor. Her deep blue eyes were riveted into the dark gray eyes of the tall man that held her arm.

Though she had always been able to attract the attention of any man she desired, never in her life had Amanda herself been captivated simply by the sight of a man. He was tall, over six feet, with a deeply tanned handsome face. He was so handsome as to almost be called pretty.

His dark brown, hair was fashionably long. His shoulders were broad, filling out his dark topcoat. In his left hand he held a brass-topped cane of some dark wood.

"You should be more careful, my dear, you could hurt yourself if you fell."

For a long moment, she was content to allow him to hold her tightly before she collected herself and pulled herself upright, moving away from his hand.

"Uh, thank you. I, uh, well I - - -" she stammered, embarrassed at finding herself tongue tied.

"Quite all right, my dear. I believe that you were asking Manuel a question when I entered the room." He said in his deep voice, as he again reached for her arm, guiding her to a nearby chair. "Perhaps I can help. Poor Manuel sometimes has trouble with his English. Please sit and join me for a few minutes."

Without waiting for her to say anything thing, he pulled a chair out from the closest table for her to sit in.

"Manuel, two hot toddies." He ordered without taking his eyes from hers.

Ignoring the chair, she half turned in protest to stop the order; she felt that she had to get to El Noche as soon as possible.

"But, I really must go," she protested starting for the door, "I have to meet my sister."

He stopped her with a broad strong hand on her arm. His steely gray eyes locked with her blue ones. He led her, without protesting, back to her table.

"Really, my dear," he soothed in a calming voice, "the storm is getting worse. Even in good weather, El Noche is hard to fine. Surely, you have time for at least one hot drink."

Amanda swayed for a moment, rubbing her forehead with her left hand. She couldn't understand why she was suddenly so tried. Almost against her wishes, she dropped back into her chair.

"Al--all right." She stammered, "But just one drink. I really do have to leave soon."

Silently, Manuel returned to place two large mugs before them. The tall stranger raised one and held it toward Amanda. Slowly, her eyes again captured by his, she took it from him and held it until he picked up the other. He raised it out toward her.

"To you, my dear." He offered in a soothing voice.

With a slightly vacant smile, Amanda raised her mug and sipped her drink. She found it almost impossible to pull her eyes away from his.

He drained his drink and placed the empty mug back on the table. With a slight smile, he leaned back in his chair, his eyes surveying Amanda as if she were a model on display for his personal viewing.

"My name is Dakkar, Simon Dakkar," he offered.

Amanda's heart was all a flutter. She couldn't understand what was going on. She had never felt such emotions before.

"Uh, I'm Amanda Bennett, from New York. I wish to thank you for your assistance. I don't know where my manners are. I'm just in such a hurry to get to my sister."

He smiled again, a narrow, thin smile.

"I am more than happy to help, my dear." He returned once again. "You were asking poor Manuel about the old town of El Noche, I believe."

"I was?" She began, for a moment she couldn't remember why she was there. It was a major effort for her to focus her thoughts, but suddenly she remembered Sheila and why she was in New Mexico.

"Oh, yes, I was. I'm to meet my sister in some little town called El Noche. But with this storm and the Interstate closed and the totally worthless map the rental company gave me, I seem to be lost."

Simon Dakkar smiled his thin smile again. "Do not feel badly my dear, El Noche is somewhat off the beaten path, but it's really not all that hard to find. Go down this road to the next intersection and turn left. Then follow that road over the mountain and take the next right. Two miles past that, you will find the little town of El Noche."

Amanda Bennett smiled as she again rose to her feet, this time in a much steadier manner, and offered Dakkar her hand.

"I do thank you Mr. Dakkar. I wish I could stay longer, but I need to be in El Noche tonight. With this storm, it will take much longer than I planned."

He rose as well and took her small hand between his two big hands.

"I understand my dear. Perhaps we will meet again."

With a final dazzling smile, Amanda regretfully pulled her hand from his and slowly, sensuously crossed the dining room to the lobby. She was well aware of his interest and felt that it was wise to keep that interest. As she walked away she could feel his eyes following her. Simon Dakkar looked and dressed as if he might have money. Possibly a potential investment client, she thought to herself.

For the first time, she noticed that the rest of the restaurant was deserted. Strange, she thought, where is everyone? The rest of dining room and the lobby were deserted, there wasn't even a cashier, she thought. Then her thoughts were pulled back to Simon Dakkar, who, when she glanced back, was still watching her from across the room.

Passing through the outer doors, Amanda paused on the front steps, under the awning. The rain was still pouring down in almost solid sheets; she could only barely see her car some twenty feet away. She was definitely in for another thorough soaking. Taking a deep breath, she dashed across the gravel, stumbling in her spike heels shoes. Finally, she jerked open the car door and virtually dove into the dryness of her car. She leaned back against the seat, catching her breath. What horrible weather, she thought, why did I ever agree to come to this state?

Reaching into her small purse, Amanda grabbed her keys and started the engine, coaxing the heater to full force. She flipped on the wipers, then leaned forward and allowed the warm air from the vents to dry the water from her face before pulling herself up in her seat, reaching for the shift lever.

Suddenly, she was pulled roughly back against the seat by her long hair, a damp cloth clamped over her mouth and nose. She could feel the arms clamped around her. Terrified, she struggled to pull away from the hands that held her so tightly, but whatever the cloth had been soaked in was working quickly. Amanda felt her strength ebbing; she saw pinpoints of light flickering before her eyes as she felt herself falling. Finally, things went dark for her as she slumped in her seat, her head falling to the side as she went completely limp.

The figure in the back seat held the cloth over Amanda's nose for a few more seconds before stuffing it into a pocket. Putting a hand beneath each of Amanda's arms, the intruder pulled his prisoner over into the passenger seat, carefully folding Amanda's long legs beneath her. With one lithe movement, the intruder almost flowed over the seat and dropped behind the wheel. The plan had worked like a charm, Amanda Bennett was a prisoner.

Whistling to himself, the kidnaper flipped on a small flashlight and placed the end between his teeth. Quickly, he pulled a small case from his pocket and propped it carefully on the dash. Raising the lid, the limited light showed that there was a single syringe nestled in between two small drug vials. Moving slowly, but surely, he took the syringe and stuck the needle into the first vial and drew off a small amount. Exchanging the first vial for the second, he drew off a small amount of that to mix with the first.

He held the syringe up to the light and taped it gently to remove any air bubbles. Reaching over, he pulled Amanda's left arm close to him and expertly injected the syringe into the vein on the inside of her elbow, mashing the plunger. Immediately, her breathing became long and slow. After a few seconds, he leaned over her and gently pushed open one eyelid, her pupils were dilated. She was thoroughly unconscious.

CHAPTER EIGHT

After glancing around to insure that no one had seen what had happened, the kidnapper placed the rental car in gear and drove slowly across the parking lot. Stopping momentarily near the black car from which he had come, the driver flicked his headlights twice. The black car answered with a single flick of its own lights and drove back to the road, turning to the left. The kidnapper followed slowly.

Settling into a safe pace, the two car caravan made its' way toward the mountains. As the rain pounded down on the roof of the car Amanda Bennett slept peacefully; totally oblivious to her surroundings. The only light to be seen in any direction was from the dash lights. By this very limited illumination, from time to time, the kidnapper glanced over at his attractive prisoner. Each glance was longer. Finally, the temptation was too much. There had been very strict instructions regarding Amanda Bennett's safety, but, he felt, no one would notice a few liberties.

Carefully keeping his eyes on the road, and one hand on the wheel, the kidnapper reached over with his right hand and pulled Amanda Bennett's jacket open, her thin dress was visible beneath it. Slowly and carefully, the roving hand began to open the row of buttons that kept the top of the dress closed. As each button was opened, more and more of the beautiful woman beneath the clothes was revealed. Eventually, the fumbling hand had opened all of the buttons, the top of the thin dress fell open revealing Amanda's full breasts to his roving hand and probing eyes, only partially covered by a thin bra. The roving hand slid slowly beneath the bra cups.

Soon the hand moved from fondling the full breasts to the hem of the fashionably short skirt. Amanda's long, limp legs were easily manipulated, the left slowly pulled straight to lie across the lap of the driver. The right leg was crumpled in the floor. The position caused her legs to be spread wide apart. Slowly, gently, the driver's hand roved across the nylon-covered leg. Each time the hand roamed up the leg, it went higher, finally going beneath the edge of the damp dress. Finally, the roving hand discovered that Amanda wore a garter belt beneath her dress; above the top of the stocking was silky smooth flesh.

Eventually temptation became too much for the kidnapper. The roving hand reached her crotch, gently the fingers insinuated themselves beneath the wispy silk panties that covered the unconscious woman below the waist. In response to the gentle manipulation of the most private area of her body, Amanda softly moaned and struggled to sit up, but fell back against the passenger door. As the car sped through the stormy night, the roving hand had its fill of Amanda Bennett's lush body.

Vaguely, she was aware that she was being violated, but the drug was so powerful that she was fighting a losing battle in her attempts to open her eyes. Slowly, Amanda felt the last of her strength slip away as she slid into a deep darkness.

A few more minutes of driving brought the cars to a paved drive that led to the right, between to large brick columns. The black car slowly drove up the long winding drive, Amanda Bennett's rental car followed obediently. Only a few minutes up the drive, the two cars entered a circular driveway before a large expensive looking house. At the front of the house was a large recessed entryway. The rental car stopped directly before the entryway where a silent figure held a lantern high.

When the rental car came to a stop, the lantern holder came forward to open the door, motioning to another figure standing in the shelter of the entry. Reaching into the car, the second figure pulled Amanda's unconscious form from the seat and carried her quickly into the house. The cars drove slowly away.

Inside the house, the one carrying Amanda mounted the stairs, taking the unconscious woman into the first open door at the top of the stairs. Carefully, he placed the woman on the bed, and hurriedly left. The door closed, leaving Amanda asleep on the bed.

A few minutes later, a tall blonde woman of indeterminate years, dressed in a short robe that showed her magnificent legs to the best effect, entered the room, a basin of water on her hands, a towel draped over one arm. A second woman came behind her, wearing only a man's dress shirt, her legs also bare, carrying a tray holding shaving gear and two syringes.

"Set your things on the table and help me," ordered the blonde.

Obediently, the second, smaller woman placed her things down and came to stand beside the bed. The blonde placed her own burdens on the bedside table and placed one knee on the bed.

"Help me!" She ordered, as she took one of Amanda's arms and pulled the unconscious woman upright.

Once again, the smaller woman obeyed the commands. Taking Amanda's other arm; she helped the blonde remove Amanda's jacket, tossing it on the floor beside the bed. As a result of Amanda's kidnapper's roving hand, the front of her dress was already unbuttoned, so it was a simple thing for the two women to peel the still damp dress from her shoulders. Now above the waist, only a small red, lacy bra partially covered Amanda's full breasts.

At a signal from the blonde, the two allowed Amanda to fall back on the bed and moved to her feet. It took only a quick movement to remove her rain-damaged shoes revealing her perfectly formed, stocking covered, small feet. The blonde then mounted the bed, sitting astride the unconscious woman. Grabbing the damp dress, with the help of her assistant, the garment was pulled completely off and tossed to the floor to join the jacket. In addition to the red bra, only a small red pair of bikini panties and a red garter belt covered Amanda's lush body.

Once again, Amanda was pulled up right, her head lolling forward, her long hair covering her face, as the second woman held her.

The blonde unsnapped the red bra and let it slide down Amanda's arms. Slowly, her hands slid around Amanda and caressed the full breasts. The blonde buried her face in Amanda's hair, inhaling her scent deeply. With her left hand, the blonde pulled Amanda's hair from her over right ear, forcing her head over to the left, exposing her long slim neck. Gently, the blonde stoked Amanda's neck, feeling for her main artery.

Smiling widely, showing her fang like incisors, the blonde held out her hand to have the smaller woman place a syringe in it. Continuing to rub gently on Amanda's artery, the blond finally found the spot she was looking for and in one quick movement, inserted the needle deeply into Amanda's neck, puncturing the main artery. Steadily, she injected the contents of the syringe into Amanda's bloodstream.

Weakly, Amanda tried to pull away from her tormentors, but the drug that put she had been injected with, still held her in its' thrall. She was also not a physical match for the two women who held her. All Amanda could do was moan softly in pain as she sank again into oblivion.

Finally, the blonde allowed Amanda to fall back on the bed and turned her attention to her prisoner's large full breasts. Her companion was stripping Amanda of her stockings, garter belt and panties. Slowly, the blonde molded and caressed the full breasts of her prisoner as she watched the smaller woman carefully wash and lather Amanda's legs prior to quickly shaving them.

By the time the two were finished with her, Amanda was beginning to rouse. She was weakly struggling as she tried to sit up. At a signal from the blonde, the smaller woman held Amanda's arms as the blonde grabbed a handful of Amanda's hair and pulling her head to one side, once again exposed her long slim neck. She clapped her other hand over Amanda's mouth and dropped into a seated position behind the prisoner to wrap her long legs around Amanda's body, pinning her arms to her side.

Quickly, the smaller woman moved to join the blonde, another syringe in her hand. While the blonde held Amanda's head to the side exposing her long slim neck, the brunette again gently stroked the main artery until she found a spot that suited her. Once again, Amanda was injected with an unknown drug. For a few seconds, she struggled wildly, but soon Amanda's struggles became weaker and weaker. Soon she lapsed into unconsciousness again.

Finally, satisfied that Amanda was again helpless, the blonde freed Amanda's head from her grip. She reached across the unconscious Amanda and grabbed a handful of her companion's hair. Pulling her close, but still gripping Amanda's body with her powerful legs, she smashed her mouth against that of her companion as she ran her hands under her companion's blouse. The smaller woman made no reaction until the blonde finished.

"Syringe," ordered the blonde as she released her grip on Amanda and moved to a position beside her.

Taking one of Amanda's arms, the blonde held it out straight, tight to her side. Carefully, she felt in the bend of the arm until she found the vein. Taking the syringe from her companion, slowly she inserted the needle and pushed the plunger. After a few minutes, the blonde pulled up one of Amanda's eyelids and carefully examined her eye to confirm that the prisoner was totally unconscious.

Satisfied, she looked at her companion.

"Rope."

Silently, the smaller woman handed the blonde a length of rope. The blonde entwined her fingers in Amanda's hair and pulled her back into a sitting position.

"Hold her!" she ordered.

The small woman grabbed a hand full of Amanda's hair and pulled her body forward. The blonde pulled Amanda's arms behind her back and carefully tied them there by running the rope around Amanda's chest, just below her full, firm breasts. Crossing Amanda's slim wrists, the blonde securely tied them before running the rope up to tie Amanda's elbows together. This method of tying her elbows together forced Amanda to almost arch her back, forcing her already large breasts to become even more prominent.

Finally satisfied with her rope work, the blonde allowed Amanda to fall back, though her tied elbows made it impossible for her to lie flat on the bed. Her full weight was resting on her elbows with her head hanging back. Crawling off the bed, the blonde took Amanda's left ankle in her hand and pulled the leg to the edge of the bed. Picking up another length of rope, she secured Amanda's ankle to the bed frame. The smaller woman was doing the same thing to Amanda's right ankle.

"One last item," stated the blonde as she picked up a wad of cloth from the floor. Sitting on the bed, she pried open Amanda's mouth and stuffed the wad of cloth securely inside, before placing a strip of cloth across her mouth and securing it tightly behind her head.

Turning to her friend, the blonde held out one hand.

"Time for bed."

Obediently, the smaller woman took the blonde's hand and followed her out of the room. Haughty Amanda Bennett was left alone, stripped, bound and gagged. Once the door closed behind the two and the lights were turned out, only the sound of the raging storm could be heard.

CHAPTER NINE

Amanda Bennett slowly came back to consciousness, aware only of intense pain in her arms and shoulders. She tried to shift her position and discovered that she couldn't move. Groggy, she opened her eyes, and found herself in a strange room, lying in the center of a large bed. It took only a few seconds for her to find out that she was tightly bound. What disturbed her the most was the fact that she could tell that she was totally nude. The possibilities disturbed her more than she was able to admit, even to herself. Surrounded by several people she didn't know, she knew that she had very little control over the situation. With a start, Amanda suddenly realized that while she was totally naked, she had no absolutely no memory of removing her clothes.

In spite of her precarious position, Amanda's ready temper flared and she struggled to pull herself loose. However, to her continual frustration, her arms were tightly bound and she wasn't able to even pull her legs together. Whoever had tied her this way had definitely known their business. Giving up, she fell back against her bound elbows. With her elbows tied together, the strain on her shoulders and ribs was tremendous. The pain was excruciating.

In spite of the pain, Amanda was beginning to doze off again when the bedroom door suddenly opened. Grunting as loudly as possible, Amanda tried to call for help. To her shock, her acquaintance from the previous night, Simon Dakkar came strolling casually into the room, still dressed impeccably. A tall blonde woman in a skintight leather jumpsuit and a smaller brunette followed him.

"Well, my dear," said Simon Dakar, "I see you have rejoined us. I do hope that you enjoyed your sleep."

"Umph," was the only sound that Amanda could force through her gag.

"My dear, you were brought here for a purpose. I wonder if you can help us. We are looking for a small golden disk about the size of a small saucer. We are aware that your father purchased such a disk at an auction house in New York. We want it!" said Simon Dakkar in his smooth voice.

Amanda was aware that someone had set down on the other side of the bed. She paid no attention to who it might be until she felt a small soft hand began to caress her right breast. Instinctively, she tried to pull away, causing herself additional pain as her weight came down fully on her bound elbows. The hand that held her breast tightened its' grip and literally pulled her back into her original position by her breast. She turned her head to meet the eyes of the hard looking attractive blonde.

"My dear, Julia is not one to take rejection calmly," commented Dakkar, "You have attracted her attention, and I am sorry to say that you might react better to my questions after a session with her."

Amanda tried to say something, but could only try to struggle and make unintelligible noise as the blonde, Julia, pushed grabbed a handful of Amanda's hair and pulled her head to the left. With her other hand, gently, she brushed back the hair covering Amanda's right ear, once again exposing Amanda's long neck. With a loud hiss, Julia buried her face in Amanda's soft neck just as she had the night before. With a quick shake of her blonde head, Julia found the proper spot and forced Amanda's torso back against her bound elbows as her incisors sank slowly into Amanda's neck. Greedily, the blonde began to feed on the flowing blood.

The unexpected pain in her neck caused Amanda to renew her struggles to try and pull away from her attacker. Her futile attempts to move her upper body caused additional pain to shoot through her arms and shoulders. The effort was useless however, as Julia's sucking mouth was firmly clamped to Amanda's long slim neck. A loud sucking sound filled the room as Julia continued to feed on the lifeblood of the struggling young woman. As she lost more blood, Amanda's struggles got weaker and weaker as she felt consciousness receding.

"That's enough, Julia," commanded Dakkar as he walked closer to the side of the bed.

With one last mouthful of warm blood, Julia obediently pulled away from Amanda, daintily wiping the blood from around her mouth with a corner of the sheet. Amanda sucked air into her lungs as best she could through her nose, as she struggled to stay conscious. Not surprisingly, she felt unbelievably weak. She was faintly aware that this position placed her assets on display, but she was in so much pain, she really didn't care.

She only vaguely noticed that the other woman had crawled between her widely stretched legs and began to gently rub her exposed crotch. The numerous conflicting sensations made it difficult for Amanda to think clearly.

"Now, my dear," began Dakkar sitting on the edge of the bed, "Once again, where is the small golden disk?"

He waited for a few minutes as Amanda regained her senses before asking his question again. Again, Amanda could only make unintelligible noises through her gag. Finally, he looked at Julia.

"Remove the gag." He ordered.

Quickly, Julia reached behind Amanda's head and untied the strip of cloth. Tossing it aside, she cupped Amanda's chin as she reached two fingers into Amanda's mouth and pulled out the wad of cloth. Amanda sucked air into her starved lungs through her open mouth.

"Now, my dear, where is the disk?" He asked again, "I must warn you that I and my superiors are not patient people. I must have an answer."

"Who are you people"? demanded Amanda, fear and rage making her voice crack. "Release me this minute! I'll sue you people for everything you've got. How dare you! Where are my clothes?"""

Simon Dakkar cupped her small chin in his powerful right hand and gently squeezed it. The pressure on her face was enormous, Amanda was soon groaning in pain.

"Amanda, you silly child, do not think to use your famous temper on me. I have tamed women much more fierce than you could ever hope to be. You are completely in my power, no one knows that you are here, no one can help you. You are totally at my mercy."

He released his grip on her chin and perched on the edge of the bed.

"I desire some information from you and, I do assure you that you will soon beg to answer my questions unless you cooperate."

He paused a moment and then gently ran a finger over her full lips. His victim tried to angrily jerk her head away from his attentions, but Julia held her hair too tightly. Amanda could barely move her head.

"Once again, I must ask you where the small golden disk is that your father purchased at auction."

"I-- I, don't know what you're talking about." Amanda responded, her long, narrow tongue flicking out of her mouth to lick her dry lips.

Dakkar shook his head sadly. He grabbed a handful of her thick hair and gently shook her head.

"Not the right answer, I am afraid. Knowing your mercenary mindset, I also find it hard to believe that you have no idea that you're father had purchased such a valuable item or where such a valuable item would be since we know that you were your father's executrix when he met his most unfortunate "accident" late last month.

We also are well aware that you father purchased the disk less than a year ago from the estate of the late Dr. Jonathan Carter when it was auctioned," he finished. "Perhaps, Julia needs to convince you again."

Amanda cringed as the blonde reached out a hand to again cup her right breast; two fingers gripped her turgid nipple. Uneasily, her eyes locked with Dakar's, she tried to pull away from the grasping hand, but the blonde's grip tightened until Amanda moaned in pain.

"No, please, I really don't know," she gasped, "I never paid any attention to what my father spent his money on. It was my sister that helped him in his collecting. If he had it before he died, then it's my sister that has it---."

Amanda's words were cut off by a deep moan as she finally gave into the pain of her pinched nipple. Julia was alternately squeezing and releasing her right breast and every so often, digging her fingernail into Amanda's rubbery nipple. Each assault sent pain shooting throughout her breast.

Leaning forward, Dakkar placed his right hand across her eyes and stared fixedly at the captive woman. Julia moved to her waist and held her legs tightly. In a few seconds, a greenish glow began to radiate from the hand that held her head.

"Amanda, you are going to answer my questions, do you hear me?"

For several seconds, the woman struggled to pull her head away from his confining hand, but finally she lay still, breathing deeply and slowly.

"Amanda," he said in a soft soothing voice. "Amanda, do you hear me?"

Moaning softly, she fought against answering, but finally, she breathed a tiny, "Yes."

Dakkar smiled a triumphant smile and glanced over his left shoulder at Julia, who was now slowly massaging the tightly stretched muscles of Amanda's full thighs. Her long supple fingers dug deeply into the straining leg muscles of the captive brunette.

"You are right, my dear, she is a fighter. Our Lord will truly enjoy this morsel."

Once again, he concentrated on the hand he had gripping her temples.

"Amanda, I want to know where the golden disk is that your father purchased. You want to tell me don't you?"

"Yes," she breathed softly, "I want to tell you."

Dakkar smiled a long slow smile, like a predator.

"Where is it, Amanda. Where is the disk?"

"My sister, Sheila, she has the disk. My father sent it to her as a birthday present."

Nodding to himself, Dakkar added additional pressure to the temples of the almost totally unconscious woman.

"Where is your sister, now?"

"In El Noche, New Mexico."

He smiled one of his feral smiles as he began to massage the throbbing temples of the captive.

"Amanda, what do you know of Asmodeus?"

"That name was on a tape made by my father the day he died." murmured Amanda.

A look of concern crossed his face, he hadn't been aware that Bennett had possibly had enough time to tell anyone of his discovery, much less make a tape recording. Such a recording could prove troublesome; he would have to take steps to obtain it.

"Amanda, who has the tape your father made?"

"The police in New York City, they are still investigating my father's death."

With a deep sigh, Dakkar removed his hand from her temples and stood up slowly. Her head fell back and her eyes fluttered rapidly for a few seconds. Finally, she closed her eyes tightly and then opened them.

"What happened?" she moaned, trying again to raise herself up. "What did you do to me?"

"Too bad, my dear, you could have joined us, but instead you chose to oppose us." said Dakkar rising from the bed, "I told you that we'd get our answers from you. You very nicely told us that your sister has what we seek. If your sister does have it, then we will have to talk to her.

Perhaps she will be more cooperative. Since you told me last night and now confirmed for me that she is in El Noche, I don't suppose we need you, now do we."

"What---what are you going to do to me?" gasped Amanda.

"We have another service that you can perform for us, since you don't have the disk," he said as he walked toward the door.

"But ----umph." began Amanda as Julia grabbed her head and

roughly stuffed the wad of cloth back into her mouth. The strip of cloth was quickly retied across her mouth to keep the gag in place.

Dakkar paused at the door and looked back at Julia who, still holding Amanda by her long hair, met his gaze with a look of expectation. Slowly, her tongue slid from her mouth to lick her ruby, red lips.

"We have time and you promised," she protested.

"Oh, very well, have your enjoyment with her, but no permanent injuries." he cautioned, pointing his cane at her, "She must be in perfect condition for the Master."

Letting go of Amanda's long tresses, Julia came around to the foot of the bed to join her friend. Slowly, Julia crawled on the bed between Amanda's widely spread legs, softly running her hands up and down her prisoner's thighs. The blonde again licked her lips in anticipation. As Dakkar closed the door behind him, he heard Amanda began to scream even though the gag as he heard the unmistakable sounds of Julia "entertaining" their guest.

The storm raged fiercely through the morning and by midafternoon it had increased its' fury. It was as dark as night, when Dakkar returned to the room that held his captive. He was somewhat earlier than needed, but he had to admit to himself that he was curious as to how Amanda had handled the demands he knew had been made on her body by Julia and her friend.

Dakkar wasn't worried that they would hurt her, for Julia had no desire to explain to the Master why Amanda was not perfect. He was fairly assured that Amanda was a healthy, lusty woman, but Amanda had been at the mercy of the two women since early morning. He wanted to see how an individual who normally dominated her partners handled being totally helpless and at the mercy of two demanding females.

Of course, he thought to himself as he entered the room, Amanda had also been considerably weakened by her trials of the previous night. He was sure that Julia had made free use of the various drugs at her disposal in having her way with Amanda. It was barely possible that the continuing demands might have been too much for her system.

Opening the door, Dakkar flipped on the lights, reassured by the sight of the blonde's smaller companion lying between Amanda's widely spread legs, her head pillowed on the captive's stomach. He could see that at some time during the day, Amanda's arms were retied so that the elbows were free, only her wrists were still secured behind her back. Her legs also had been untied, though they were still spread widely apart, held so by the body of the girl lying between her legs.

It appeared to him that Amanda, herself, was either asleep or unconscious. Walking closer to the bed, Dakkar noticed a large reddish spot on Amanda's neck so he rightly assumed that she was just unconscious from either loss of blood or one injection too many. Julia had also fallen asleep with her mouth still on Amanda's turgid right nipple.

From the captive's sweat matted hair and the musty odor in the room, it appeared to Dakkar that Amanda had endured a rather strenuous afternoon with the two women. He was well aware of their various sexual appetites. He smiled to himself, wishing he had the time to have the captive himself, but he had more important fish to fry.

"Julia, it is time to prepare her," he commanded softly, leaning over the sleeping blonde.

Stretching lazily like a big cat, the blonde opened her eyes and looked up at Darker.

"I want her beautiful for the festivities tonight, Julia." he commanded. "From the looks of things, it will take the two of you some little time to prepare her."

Languidly, Julia rose to her knees on the bed and smiled; her red tinted fangs still prominent in her mouth. Slowly she ran her hand over Amanda's face and hesitated over her neck area.

"There is no time for any more of that, Julia," cautioned Dakkar. "She must be alert for tonight's ceremony. I certainly do hope that you have controlled your appetites. Too much drug use and blood loss and the Master will not be pleased."

"Oh. Simon, she was wonderful. Her blood had a very good bouquet and she was incredibly responsive," purred Julia, leaning over to lick delicately at the bloody spot on Amanda's neck. "She is strong willed and a real fighter, but once I had her in position and applied the proper pressure, she gave in to me completely. She opened herself and submitted to me. She's worth the effort.

"I really wish you had caught her earlier so that I could have had some more time with her. I'm sorry that she has to be used in such a fashion. She's the best I have ever had."

Dakkar walked over to the bed and stood towering over the captive. He was concerned that the two women might have marked her body in some fashion, but he could see only one or two bruises.

"Get her ready, Julia. If she is that good, then the Master will really enjoy her. He hasn't been truly satisfied in a long time."

Julia reached into a drawer of the bedside table and pulled out a small bottle of ammonia, which she waved under Amanda's nose. Grunting and moaning, Amanda returned to slowly to consciousness. Julia grabbed a hand full of her long hair and jerked her head up enough to force a pillow under it. Amanda awoke with a start, trying to sit up before Julia controlled her by grabbing her sore right breast. In response, Amanda moaned and tried to twist away. She struggled to pull her legs together, but the smaller brunette slapped Amanda's full thighs and jerked the captive's legs open again. Amanda fell back against the bed, breathing hard, eyes flashing.

"Back with us, I see." Dakkar smiled slowly, leaning forward to trace her lower lip with his right index finger. "I trust, from what I see that you enjoyed the afternoon."

Amanda made no sound, but merely lay panting on the bed and glared her rage. In her anger, Amanda seemed to pay no attention to either Julia's roaming hands or the brunette lying between her widely spread thighs.

"I hope you have enjoyed our hospitality, for now you must pay the final bill," said Dakkar, as he walked around the bed, viewing her naked body from all angles. There was no question that she was a truly beautiful woman. He had a moment of regret that she was not for him.

For a moment, Amanda's expression was one of puzzlement. It was obvious that she was trying to understand his references to "paying the bill". Dakkar smiled again as he pushed her chin up with the tip of his cane.

"How are you going to pay the bill?" he said softly, as if talking to himself, "Why it's very simple my dear. You will be the main of attraction at a little get together this evening. You will be stripped, fondled and fooled with by all and then as the final act, you will be sacrificed to the Dark God, Asmodeus. You will die tonight."

He paused and pulled aside the curtains to glance out at the storm. He could feel his Master's power radiating from his underground prison, so close and yet so far away from this house. In the direction that Dakkar was looking was El Noche Valley and Devil's Hill, the location of the magical prison of his Dark Lord.

Spinning around, he looked at Julia.

"No more delays. Prepare her," he ordered as he left the room.

Swiftly, Julia and her assistant untied the captive woman and jerked her to her feet. This was the first time that Amanda's arms had been free since her capture. She had been tied and drugged for so long that her legs immediately buckled and she almost fell. Like a cat, Julia was on Amanda's back, twisting her arms behind her. Her wrists were, once again, firmly secured and she was hauled back to her feet, to be half carried and half led to the bathroom.

Faced with her own death, helpless, friendless, Amanda began to cry, at first softly, then as loud as the gag would allow. Being bound, gagged and abused as she had been, her hopes for escape were fading rapidly. Her situation was hopeless.

The fight gone, she stood obediently and allowed the two women to bathe, perfume and powder her aching body. Her arms were retied in front of her and her wrists tied to a ring in the ceiling of the shower. Still at their mercy, Amanda was thoroughly scrubbed by both of them; her long hair washed and shampooed until it was squeaky clean. Finally, after being forced to sit in a small chair, her makeup was carefully applied. When they were finished, even she had to admit that she had never looked more beautiful, a beautiful sacrifice.

PART THREE

THE SACRIFICE

CHAPTER TEN

After being made up, Amanda was returned to the bed, to get her "beauty sleep", as the blonde bitch called it. When she resisted being placed back on the bed, her hair was used as an extra leverage to force her onto her back.

By the bedside clock, Amanda could tell that it was almost midnight, when her "hosts" came and freed her from the bed. For only the second time since she had awakened, Amanda's arms were untied. For several hours that afternoon, after she had been washed, shampooed and perfumed, her arms and legs had been thoroughly massaged and her hair brushed until it gleamed.

Finally satisfied with their efforts to improve her appearance, her captors had brought her back to the bedroom and forced her to, again, lie on her back and spread her arms and legs. Rapidly, her wrists and ankles had been tied to the bed frame. While she had been in the bathroom, someone had changed the bed covers for silk sheets.

Once she had been firmly secured and gagged, Julia had crawled into the bed with her and nuzzled her throat with her lips.

"We'll just sleep a little until time to go," purred the blonde, plastering herself against Amanda's helpless body.

Amanda noticed that the blonde's friend had left the room. Amanda had lain quietly allowing the blonde to cuddle her until a little after eleven. At that time the smaller brunette had returned carrying several bundles. The blonde had untied Amanda while the small brunette had forced a folded black garment in her numb hands.

"Put this on!" she had snapped.

Determined to cooperate until she could find a way to escape, Amanda obediently slipped her arms into the garment, to find that she had donned a long black robe that covered her from her throat to her feet. A cowl hung down the back. She was then handed a length of cord to use as a belt. She looked like some kind of a monk.

Suddenly, Amanda tried to make a break for the door. Her unexpected attack had knocked the smaller brunette from her feet, but Julia had been alert for such a move. Like a bird, Julia had literally flown across the room to wrap her long muscular arms around Amanda's knees. The two had crashed to the floor just inside the bedroom door, with Amanda on the bottom.

With unbelievable speed and agility, Julia had immediately twisted Amanda's left arm behind her back while the other woman joined them to help secure her wrists. Another rope looped around her neck served as a very serviceable leash. In this fashion, she was forced to her feet, hustled through the house and out to the garage.

Prior to forcing her into the car, Julia placed a blindfold securely across her Amanda's eyes. Freezing, for the outside air and rain coming under the partially opened garage door was bitterly cold and she was naked under the robe; afraid to move for fear of falling, Amanda had no choice but to allow herself to be pushed into the car. Two other persons crawled in behind her.

When the motor started, Amanda was forced to kneel on the floorboard, her head forced down onto the seat so that no one outside the car could see her. Someone kept their hands on her upper back at all times. She heard someone get in the front passenger seat and heard the car doors slam shut. Finally, she felt the car back slowly out of the garage and head down the drive.

At first, the gentle rumble of the car and the continual sound of the rain on the roof as it moved down the road lulled Amanda's senses. In spite of her situation, Amanda began to become drowsy. She was struggling to stay awake when she felt a small hand slip inside the robe to close on one of her full breasts. It was the same breast that Julia had worked on all afternoon so it was quite sore. Amanda tried to pull away, but the hand clamped down tightly, squeezing the nipple into a point. In spite of herself, Amanda let out a loud moan.

Another person in the back seat with her grabbed Amanda by her chin and pulled her head back, once again exposing her now, sore, throat. Slim fingers began to massage her neck. Her hair that had fallen forward over her face was pulled aside and her head was forced to the side allowing the unseen person access to Amanda's long slim neck.

She also felt a soft hand slid down her stomach toward her crotch area. Tied as she was, there was nothing Amanda could do to protect herself, so she was forced to, again, submit to the desires of her captors. She was so tired and discouraged that she had absolutely no thoughts of resisting. Amanda went limp and just let the hands do as they wished with her battered body. Her last ride, she thought, as once again her tears began to flow, and being molested was just one additional dignity.

The scene was so strange as to have been lifted from a B horror movie. They had entered a cave in a brushy hillside. Firelight flickered in the dimness of the cavern. Numerous scarlet robed figures filled one side of the vastness, standing in orderly rows. Standing on a low dais in front of the group, facing them, was a giant figure, its' form partially shrouded by the shadows that filled the room. Before the giant figure, was a low slab carved from a block of living stone.

The sound of a loud gong filled the cavern. From the group of robed figures came a low chant.

"Asmodeus, Asmodeus," they chanted.

After a few moments, one of the scarlet robbed figures in the front row stepped forward, and threw out his arms toward the giant figure. The hood fell back revealing the face of Simon Dakar.

"O Prince of Darkness, come to us. Lead us in returning this world to the chaos that existed when the world was young. To a time when you and your lesser brothers walked among us and our order followed your lead. Come to us in our hour of need!"

Falling silent, the leader of the robed ones nodded to someone in the shadows. Slowly a procession of four robed figures came forward leading a stumbling, struggling dark clad figure. At another signal from the leader, two of the procession lit large torches, bathing the group in a pool of light. It was now clear that the stumbling figure was a bound and gagged woman.

The procession halted, two of the robed figures jerked the bound figure around to face the leader, who raised his arms to the giant figure.

"O Asmodeus, except this offering to show our adoration and belief in your mighty powers."

Another nod to the two guardians of the prisoner brought them into motion. As one they ripped the mask and gag from the smaller prisoner. The mass of dark hair that fell free at the removal of the mask showed that the prisoner was a young woman.

"Who are you people?" Amanda Bennett screamed, struggling to escape from her captors, "What do you want with me? You have no right to do this to me."

At another silent nod from the leader, the two guards grabbed the loose black robe that covered the prisoner and ripped it free so that she stood naked before the assembled group. Her magnificent body was displayed for all to see. The torches lit the area behind her, while the firelight flickered across the muscles of her flat belly and her full, proud, rosy tipped breasts. Her legs were long and slim, like those of a showgirl. What could be seen of her face showed that she was of unsurpassed beauty.

Amanda Bennett had been the center of attention at many events in her young life, but none had been as important to her as this one. She was praying that someone in the assembled crowd would come to her rescue. To her horror, she saw that the few faces she could see reflected an almost fanatical enthusiasm to see her sacrificed.

Finally, the horror the situation was too great for her. Amanda's mind snapped. Shrieking in fear, Amanda struggled even harder to pull loose from her captors. Effortlessly, the two lifted her by her bound arms and slammed her on her back on the rock table. The leader walked quickly to the head of the table, while the guards held her arms out straight to either side. As if in benediction, the leader pressed his two hands on the girl's head and bowed his head.

At a signal to his two assistants, a large black cloth was raised before the altar and then lowered to cover the struggling sacrifice.

"O Great Asmodeus, please except this, our offering to you."

Pulling the victim's head to the left side, Dakkar exposed her long slim neck. It was clear that the woman was obviously now aware of what he intended to do to her, for she tried to jerk her head back to cover her throat, but in her weakened condition, she was no match for the big man. Easily, he forced her head back to one side.

Opening his mouth wide, Dakkar showed that he, too, also had fang like incisors, though obviously artificial. With one swift movement, he bit into the woman's long slim neck and began to drain her of her life's blood. Her struggles became weaker and weaker, as the loss of blood forced her ever closer to the final darkness of death. At the last minute, Dakkar pulled away from her and called out to his god.

"O Asmodeus. Receive this gift of beauty for your use as you see fit."

Lifting his right hand, Dakkar plucked a long bladed knife from within his robe. As he held it high above his head, the firelight flickered off the long narrow blade. For several minutes, Dakkar recited an incantation, as the intended sacrifice struggled weekly to free herself from his grasp. Unable to free herself, but not really understanding her danger, she shrieked out her terror as she weakly swung her legs and continued in her attempt to jerk her arms free so that she could crawl from the altar.

"No, you can! No, don't." she moaned.

Ignoring his prisoner's struggles and pleas, the leader increased his pressure on her head, effortlessly holding her down upon the altar. Slowly, he ran his hands down her tear streaked face to cup her full breasts for a long moment, causing a fresh round of weak shrieks as he squeezed and fondled the already sore areas. Finally, tiring of her screaming, the leader grabbed a handful of her thick black hair and pulled her head back, once again exposing her soft slim throat.

"Asmodeus, except our gift!" screamed the leader and the knife flashed in the light. In mid note, the shrieks stopped, there was only one last gurgle. Blood spurted high into the air as others rushed forward the catch the fresh blood in what looked like golden chalices. The chanting grew into an unholy racket as the watchers raised their voices in worship of the God Asmodeus.

Suddenly as if a switch had been thrown the cavern grew silent. There was not a signal sound as everyone froze in place. Each person in the cavern strained to listen, but at first heard nothing. Finally, there was a faint sound like leaves blowing across a floor, which became slowly more noticeable. Then it was clear that the sound was of some great beast breathing.

"I -- am -- here," came a rumbling voice from the very air around them, "I - am - your God - I - am - Asmodeus. What do you wish?"

PART FOUR
THE STORM

CHAPTER ELEVEN

Zeke Marsters tossed the last of the nightly hay ration over the railing to his prize bull. With the weather acting as odd as it had been, he wanted nothing to happen to baby, as he called the thousand pound steer. This bull had cost him a small fortune, but it was the major piece in his master plan to increase the bloodline of his herd. Leaning the pitchfork against the wall, Zeke leaned over the rail and rubbed the young bull's face.

"You stay in here and stay warm, my friend. I'll make sure that you don't catch no cold or nothing. Come spring, you and those lady heifers out back will have a high old time."

As if he could understand his owner, the young bull made a noise deep in his throat and continued to munch on the hay piled before him. Pulling his coat tight around him, Zeke stomped over to the open doorway and stared out into the rainy night. He had never seen rain coming down with such force.

"Forty days and forty nights of rain destroyed the world once before. I bet with this much rain, we could do it in twenty." The old man muttered to himself as he shivered in the cold.

Pulling his collar up and his hat down on his baldhead, Zeke slogged his way through the mud to the end of the sprawling cattle barn. He had forty head of prime heifers in the rear pen and it was his habit to check on them each night before going to bed. Tonight, with the weather as bad as it was, he was tempted to skip checking on them, but he knew that he'd never sleep peacefully unless he made his usual nightly round.

Pulling a small flashlight from his coat pocket, Marsters lit his way across the muddy farmyard to the rear pen. The wind and rain made so much noise that he didn't know that anything was wrong until he had reached the gate to the holding pen. Normally, on stormy nights, the cattle would bunch up near the gate; waiting for him to come by and give them some of the hay it was his custom to keep nearby. On this night, he saw none of the cows.

Concerned about his herd, Marsters swung the gate open and stepped into the enclosure; he still could see none of the forty odd cattle that should have filled the enclosed area. Straining his eyes, Zeke took a few steps forward and went sprawling face down in the mud when he tripped over something on the ground.

With a curse, Zeke felt around until he could find his flashlight, which was absolutely covered with mud. Wiping the lens clean with the edge of his jacket, Zeke rose to his knees and turned the weak beam of light on the object he had stumbled over. To his horror, he was looking at part of one of his cattle, its body literally ripped in half.

Suddenly aware of the fact that it was very dark and he was weaponless and alone Zeke scrambled to his feet and flashed the light rapidly around the pen. Now that he had an idea of what to look for, he could see that there were pieces of cow littering the area, much of what he had believed was muddy water, was in fact blood and water mixed together. The pen reeked of death.

Zeke stood stunned with no idea of what to do, when he heard a sound from the barn so loud that it could be heard over the sounds of the storm. Lowering his head, Zeke frantically ran through the storm to the entrance to the barn. The big double doors were ripped from their hinges and lying in the mud some twenty feet from the building.

Heedless of his own danger, Marsters charged into the barn, frantic to protect his baby. Suddenly he skidded to a stop, his mouth hanging open with shock. Standing before the gate to the bull's stall was the most gruesome creature Marsters' had ever seen. The creature was huge, the top its' bony head towering above Marsters' own baldpate.

The thing was mottled green, with the wings of a bat, but shaped similar to those of an eagle. It had four legs, each one ending in talons such as an eagle would have. Zeke knew that those talons had been the weapons that had ripped his cattle to shreds. However, those talons were not the true horror, he saw that when the thing turned its head to face him.

The monster had a head and horns like a goat, with glowing red eyes. The face was almost human life, with two eyes, a normal nose, a wide mouth filled with razor sharp teeth and a beard like a tiger. The worst thing was that in those glowing red eyes was intelligence that rivaled that of a man. Zeke Marsters faced his death, but he couldn't let his baby die without a struggle. He would fight and he would die, the cycle of the Piasa would begin again.

Encouraged by the fact that the creature hadn't moved, Zeke ran across the barn and grabbed the pitchfork that he had used earlier to toss the hay into the stall.

"Get back you bloody great beast!" he yelled, brandishing the weapon between them. "You'll not have my baby."

It was impossible that the creature actually understood the old farmer, but Marsters felt that, at some level, the creature had actually understood his words. The wide mouth opened in something approaching a grin. Spreading his wings, the creature moved slowly toward the farmer.

In spite of himself and his demonstrated defiance, Marsters backed slowly toward the wall behind him, the pitchfork held at the ready. Finally, when his back came up against the immovable barn wall, Marsters knew that he had no choice. It was either now or never.

With a savage yell, Marsters rammed the lethal pitchfork into the broad chest before him. The sensation was the same as if he had rammed it with all his strength into a brick wall. The placid expression of the face of the creature never changed. Almost languidly, one of the mighty wings slapped the farmer across the head, knocking him from his feet. The pitchfork was sent flying through the air to land, sharply pointed tines down, in the dirt before the open doors.

Rearing up on its rear two legs, the creature reached out with the front legs to grab Marsters by his shoulders, the razor sharp talons sinking deeply into the muscles of his shoulders. Marsters screamed in pain as he was effortlessly lifted from his feet by the creature. The creature ignored both his captive's struggles and his screams, but after examining him for a moment, he tossed the old man aside. The force of the toss was sufficient to send the old man completely through the wall of the barn.

Zeke Marsters partially raised himself on one arm, but his strength finally gave out and he fell back into the mud. His last sight was of the creature flying across his line of vision, Marsters' baby clutched in those powerful talons. Then Zeke Marsters' eyes closed forever.

CHAPTER TWELVE

Fred Santos settled himself, with a long sigh, in the old cane bottom chair outside the front door of the Seven Brother's Trading Post, the main business left in El Noche, New Mexico. Wiping his mouth with a dirty red bandanna, he took a pull from the long necked bottle of cerveza he held in his right hand. The ice-cold beer cut the dust that felt like it caked his throat. It was midafternoon and high hot winds had been blowing steadily from the west, sending waves of gritty sand across the desert and the temperature soaring. Each gust of wind seemed to have more force behind it.

He didn't enjoy being out in the wind, but it was still better than being cooped up in the stifling Trading Post listening to the waves of gritty desert sand peppering the side of the low adobe building. At least outside he could watch for anyone fool enough to be out in the high winds. He had hoped that some of his friends would be in town and come sit a spell with him, but nothing moved on the dusty streets of El Noche, only a few tumbleweeds blew about in the ever-increasing wind.

The wind kept up a high pitched keening sound as it blew across the old city square, but suddenly he heard a loud banging from down the street. Busy with his own thoughts, Santos had not initially noticed the sound, but when he became conscious of it, he leaned forward to peer down the street, trying to find the source of the noise.

At first he dismissed it as somebody's shutter banging in the wind, but it stopped and started. Seeing nothing to account for the sound, Santos put down his beer and stepped from the low porch where he sat. Trying to protect his eyes from the sand blowing about, he slowly walked up the street toward the sound. Finally, he spotted the source, a few doors down. Old Doctor Markin, the only physician left in the valley, was putting shutters over his windows, hammering them solidly into place with long nails.

"Doc! Hey Doc!" bellowed Santos, trying to be heard over the keening of the wind.

"What! Who's that?" demanded the Doctor, swinging around, hammer held up like a weapon, one hand protecting his eyes from the blowing sand. His look was fearful as he began to edge along the wall toward the door to his office.

"What's the matter, you old fool? Fraid o' your own shadow now?" cackled Santos, slapping his thigh in high humor.

Doc Markin glared his anger, as he shook his hammer toward the storekeeper.

"Damn you Fred Santos, I ain't got no time for your foolishness right now, it's only a few hours until dark. I got to get ready and you should, as well, if you know what's good for you!"

Santos snorted and waved the man's advice away, "I ain't lived these seventy odd years trembling at my own shadow like the rest o'ya in this town. Old Scratch wants me; he'll have to get past my old .44. I'll shoot his eyes out he comes around me and mine. That's what I'll do; I'll shoot his mean ole eyes out."

Doc Markin snorted as he grabbed for his hat, which threatened to sail away in the wind.

"Sure you will, Fred, just like your brother Ben said he was gonna do all those years ago. He was twenty years younger than you are and a hell of a good shot. When Old Scratch attacked his ranch, he leveled the place. Old Scratch got him before Ben could fire a shot and if you don't take care, he'll get you."

Pride wounded, Fred Santos, last of the fighting Santos brothers drew himself up to his full height and pointed one bony finger at the Doctor.

"Let me tell you something Bob Markin, me and mine were

fighting to defend our homes when you were going to that dad blamed school o'yourn learnin your doctoring. Hell, we was fighting Mexicans, Injuns and anyone else that tried to take this valley long before you was born. We's still here, I survived it all. Ain't no damn haint gonna scare me away from my home."

Doctor Markin waved the angry old man away as he turned back to pounding his shutters into place.

"Ain't got time to listen to no more of your foolishness, you old fool. I got to get these shutters up. You best look to putting up your own shutters. Weather man says the wind will hit a hundred and fifty miles per hour tonight," responded the doctor, not working away from his work.

Santos stood and glared at the old Doctor for several long moments. How dare that youngster question the courage and fighting ability of a Santos. Shore, Fred was not as young as he had been the last time he had fired a shot in anger, but he still could defend himself.

With a last shake of his head, muttering to himself, Santos strode back to his chair, picked up his bottle and stomped back inside the Trading Post. In spite of his bravado, he was worried. For the past twenty years, ever since them Yankee soldier boys left the old base in the hills, there had been something that arrogantly roamed the night, killing animal and people alike. No one ever saw it, but its tracks could be found all over the valley.

In its wake, the creature or whatever it was always left death and destruction. Usually the dead were from the outlying ranches, but these last few years, whatever it was had actually come into town. Five years before, it had killed a deputy sheriff. Unfortunately, neither the Sheriff's Department nor the hounds they brought could ever track the creature. Whenever the Santa Ana winds blew as they were now blowing, the creature killed, it was time.

Santos started into the storeroom, but turned with a start as he heard the front door open. He tensed slightly at the sight of his visitor; one of them was that damn black robe from that old Mission up on Devil's Hill, near the old base. As the only source for supplies between Las Cruces and El Paso, the Mission always purchased any needed supplies from his store and as such, they represented a large source of his income. Even so, Santos found it difficult to deal with any of them holy rollers; they never spoke, communicating by written messages.

Being a blunt direct sort, Santos hated dealing with someone whose face he couldn't see. The inhabitants of the ancient Spanish Mission always wore robes and kept their faces covered by large hoods. At least those scientists that were working at the Mission had the good sense to wear real clothes.

When he noticed the second customer enter behind that damn black robe, his forced smile broadened into a real genuine smile that threatened to crack the seams in his weather-beaten face. Sheila Bennett was one of his favorite people. Straightening his rumpled shirt Santos walked over to meet his customers by the counter.

"Well howdy do, Miss Sheila. How you and the rest o'your friends doing in this weather?" he asked.

"Good morning, Mr. Santos." responded Sheila Bennett, pulling the watch cap from her head to let her mass of crimson hair free. "I guess we're as fine as can be expected. This weather has gotten worse by the hour. We wanted to get some supplies before the weather got so bad we couldn't get out."

Fred Santos glanced toward the front windows where the sand and rain continued to beat a rapid tattoo.

"Ain't never seen nothing like it in all my born days, Miss Sheila. I've seen storms before, but this one is like nothing else. Well, better let you get back before the weather worsens, what supplies do you need?

As usual, the silent black robed figure didn't speak, but simply raised an arm, a folded note protruded from under the sleeve of the robe. The hand couldn't be seen, only the proffered note. Gingerly, Santos reached across the counter and took the note. Pulling his reading glasses from his vest pocket, Santos adjusted them on his nose and unfolded the note.

"Let's see," he mumbled, "I see that you want the usual, flour, corn, bread and that sort of stuff. But---what's this here?"

Santos reached over and turned on a lamp that sat on the edge of the counter to his right. Holding the note closer to the lamp he concentrated on the fine print on the page.

"Says here that you have a visitor coming, and want me to bring her to the Old Mission."

He glanced up to see the Black Robe nod slowly. Well, at least it was a start.

"Yes sir," responded Sheila, "The visitor's my sister Amanda. She's coming from New York. According to her plans, she would have flown into Albuquerque and then was to rent a car and drive here."

"When's she supposed to be here, tomorrow?"

Sheila shook her lovely head.

"No, she's due to be here today, but we don't want to have someone wait in town for her in case the road to the Mission gets impassable due to the storm."

Santos glanced out the window; it was late afternoon and almost dark already due to the weather. In spite of his bravado before the doctor and his scoffing at the old legends, Santos had no intention of being caught outside after dark.

"Well, much as I would like to help you out, Miss Sheila, if your sister gets here after dark, there ain't no one in this town that will bring her out to that spooky old place."

A puzzled frown on her heart shaped face, Sheila leaned forward, her palms resting firmly on the beaten old wooden counter. Her eyes bored into Fred Santos'.

"But why not? Granted the weather's terrible, but why wouldn't someone help her get up to us. There's plenty of 4 wheel drive vehicles in town that would have no trouble making it up the old road to the Mission. You've got one yourself."

Santos shrugged uncomfortably, a reddish tinge discoloring his weather beaten cheeks.

"Well ma'am, to tell you the truth, there's reasons why nobody wants to go up there after dark."

"What reasons?" pressed Sheila, her eyes lighting with curiosity, "surely you're not afraid of those old stories about the Mission."

"Well, now, Miss, there are things best not gone into --------"

"This is the devil's time. When the wind blows like this, the devil's creatures walk this land after darkness falls," interrupted a low voice from behind Santos.

The old man whirled around to see an old Indian standing in the shadows just inside the corridor leading back to the Santos' living quarters.

"Hush, you old fool!" snapped Santos. "You ain't got no idea what you're talking about."

"The devil?" questioned Sheila, turning her gaze on the Indian.

Santos snorted and threw the list of supplies toward the old Indian.

"Damn Injun superstitious mumbo jumbo, if you ask me." he said to Sheila.

"I don't pay you to run your fool mouth, old man." He snapped turning back to the Indian. "Fill that list for these nice folks, Ringo."

From where he stood in the shadows, the old Indian dressed in faded jeans and a long sleeved Pendleton shirt, came shuffling through the doorway. The long dark hair framing the weather-beaten face was heavily streaked with silver. A gaily-decorated robe was draped around his bony shoulders. Silently, he took the paper from Santos and began to gather the order. He made absolutely no sound as he moved around the store placing the required items on the counter. The Black Robe, as usual, stood silently waiting for the order to be filled.

While Ringo filled the order, Santos entered his little office, directly behind the counter; he didn't notice the girl follow him.

"Mr. Santos, what was he talking about? The Indian, I mean. What kind of devil?"

Santos swiveled his old chair around to face the doorway and the lovely young lady.

"Weren't nothing but Indian superstitions, like I said. The local Indians that lived in this part of the state had all kind of legends about some type of devil that was supposed to live somewhere in this valley.

According to the old stories, the devil creature has the power to release some kind of monsters that kill all those that don't believe in him and his power."

She was instantly captivated at his stories. Like her father, history was her life and her first love.

"Has anybody ever seen these monsters?"

Santos shook his grizzled old head.

"If anybody has actually seen any monsters then they've kept the news to themselves. I do remember my daddy telling me that he once tracked some kind of strange animal up into the mountains between here and White Sands. But he never did catch sight of what he was tracking."

"Tell her of Randolph." came a voice from inside the store.

Sheila looked back over her shoulder to see the old Indian standing a few feet behind her, a ten-pound sack of flour in his gnarled left hand. His eyes were bright and alive, however, drawing her like twin pools of darkness.

"Damn you, Ringo. Randolph ain't none o'your business. I pay you to fill orders, not gossip with customers. 'Sides all that Injun spirit stuff is god damn poppycock. Ain't nothing to it," yelled the old man, his temper rising at the mention of his dead brother.

"Who's Randolph?" asked Sheila curiously, turning back to Santos.

Santos sat for a long time in what appeared to be a battle with himself. Sheila decided he wasn't going to answer, and turned back to her companion at the counter. When it came, Santos' answer was so low, she wasn't sure he had really answered her.

"Randolph Santos was my older brother."

Sheila stopped and turned back to stand again in the doorway to the small office.

"Your older brother? What's so mysterious about your older brother? You acted so strangely when the Indian mentioned his name. Why?"

She hadn't heard Ringo come up behind her.

"He fought the devil creature and he lost."

CHAPTER THIRTEEN

"Damn you, Ringo." said Santos in an empty voice. "Why can't you just let it alone?"

With shaking hands, Santos opened an ornately carved cabinet set against one wall and removed a partially empty bottle of whiskey. Removing the cap, Santos tilted the bottle back and drew off at least half of the bottle's contents. Belching loudly, he wiped his mouth with his left hand as he sat the bottle carefully down in the center of the cluttered desk.

"I haven't spoken of this to anyone for many years. In fact, it's only old folks like Ringo that even remember that there ever was a Randolph Santos or a Sarah Fuentes."

"Who's Sarah Fuentes?" asked Sheila softly, recognizing the she had inadvertently lanced a festering wound in the old man's mind.

With a deep sigh, Santos leaned back in his chair and motioned for Sheila to sit on the moth eaten couch to the left of the doorway.

"Well, I guess it can't do any harm to tell you to story." he leaned forward, resting his elbows on his knees.

"Randolph Santos was my oldest brother, actually my half-brother. He was fifteen years my senior. Don Randolph, as we called him, was everything good in life. He was tall, handsome, and the fastest man with a gun since Billy the Kid. He was-------he was my idol."

Sheila was surprised and slightly embarrassed for him when tears began to run down the old man's face.

"What happened to him?" asked Sheila softly, leaning forward to rest one of her soft hands on the old man's arm.

Suddenly, aware that he was actually crying in front of someone, Santos quickly wiped his eyes with the sleeve of his Pendleton shirt.

"It happened about sixty years ago, in the spring of 1933. I was ten at the time. Randolph was my father's first son by his first wife. My mother was his second wife. As you might guess, my father was much, much older than my mother. He married her when she was fifteen; I was born the next year."

"What happened to his first wife?"

Santos took a deep sigh and reached for the bottle to take another long drink of the burning whiskey.

"That's what started it, at least for this family."

His dark eyes stared at a spot on the wall just above Sheila's head. She somehow knew that he was looking back over the years to his youth.

"My father, Raymond Santos, was from below the border. He came here in his early teens with his father and several vaqueros. They arrived in this area in 1871, only a few years after the end of the American Civil War. This country was in still ruins; many had died in the fighting on both sides. Ranches were abandoned, cattle ran wild in the Milpas, and the Indians were beginning their last hurrah. It was a time during which an enterprising man could make a fortune.

"My father and grandfather rounded up many of those strays and started the Rocking S, the family ranch, at the south end of El Noche Valley. They had decided to settle in this valley since this was one place, in fact the only place in the territory, where the Apaches would not come. When the Hunters Moon filled the sky and the tribes raided across the Mexican Border, the Apache's would devastate every living human north of the border, except for this one valley. This allowed my family to build a large fortune."

Sheila interrupted with a question.

"Why wouldn't the Indians raid this valley?"

"My father was in his late thirties when he decided it was time to start a family," continued the old man. "Attracted by the wealth and power of the Santos family and the proven safety from Indian attacks, many other old Mexican families had moved into the valley area. One of the families was the Chavez family. The head of that family was Don Eduardo Chavez, a distant relative of the Spanish ruling family.

Many of the better families that had moved into the area hoped that my father, the heir to the Santos fortune would marry their eligible daughters. Though he had courted many, he had married none. Then in 1900, there was a fiesta held in Las Cruces. My father and his relations made the long journey to attend. During the festivities, he caught sight of Don Eduardo and his wife and daughter. From that moment on, he could see no one but Rosa Chavez.

She was a beauty. Though, naturally I never had a chance to see her, I have seen pictures which show that she was a world class beauty."

Santos stopped talking, reaching into the cabinet in which he kept his secret stash of liquor and pulled out a very old picture, showing a stunning young lady dressed in an outdated mode. Reverently, he handed it to Sheila.

"Though Rosa Chavez was only fourteen when she and my father met, my father was not a man to be denied. For Rosa, it is love at first sight. In 1902, my father married her and they built a grand home in Mesilla. When my grandfather died in 1910, my father and his bride moved from Mesilla to the Santos Ranch.

According to what I have heard, the marriage was a very happy one. My father worshipped the ground that she walked on and, in turn, she placed him at the center of her world. The only thing that was lacking was a child. That came in 1903 when Rosa had twins, Randolph and Rita, my half-sister."

Santos stopped talking, his eyes again taking on a vacant look. Sheila glanced through the doorway into the store and saw that the order had been filled. Her companion stood quietly by the window, watching the rainfall. She knew that she should leave, but she was too interested.

"What happened?" she prompted softly.

"When Randolph was fifteen, that would have been 1913, his grandfather Don Eduardo, became seriously ill and asked to see his grandchildren. Rosa was pregnant again and as often happened to pregnant women in those days; she was not in the best of health. The doctor decided that it would not be good for her to travel. So it was decided that my father and Randolph would go immediately and as soon as Rosa was able to travel, Rosa and Rita would follow.

Now remember that this was still a wild part of the country in those days. It was just three years after this that Villa attacked Columbus, New Mexico. So there was some danger involved in such a trip. Cars were not practical here in those days, so it was either wagon or horseback. My father and Randolph went by horseback, with a sizable escort of vaqueros and Rosa and Rita would come later by wagon.

When Rosa didn't arrive within a reasonable time, her father became concerned and asked my father to go see if Rosa was safe. My father dispatched several of his men back to the ranch to check on things. These men met messengers dispatched from the valley to bring him word that he needed to come back immediately.

Don Eduardo sent many of his men with my father so he arrived at the ranch with a small army behind him. The ranch house was almost destroyed; the massive front doors to the courtyard had been ripped from their hinges and tossed aside. The bodies of my father's vaqueros who had been left to guard Rosa and Rita were scattered about the house, all dead. My father found the body of Rita literally ripped to pieces in her bedroom. He never found the body of his beloved wife.

My father's men were expert trackers. They found unusual tracks in the courtyard and followed them across the valley until they lost the trail on the slope of Devil's Hill. My father never recovered from the death of his beloved Rosa. He grieved for her until his death in 1960."

"What happened to your brother?" asked Sheila.

"Randolph swore to find and kill whatever had killed his mother, sister and friends. From the day he returned to the Ranch, he began to practice with his .44 until his draw was like greased lightning. He haunted the hills searching for those tracks that had been found around the house."

"Did he find them?" she asked.

Santos nodded his head slowly.

"Oh, yes, he found them. He covered every inch of this valley looking for the lair of the creature. He found that there were patterns to the creature's appearance. He also discovered the creature was most active during October. In fact his mother and sister were killed on October 31.

However, his search never led him to anything of importance. The tracks always led him to Devil's Hill and then disappeared. Then he met the old one."

"The old one?" she asked.

Santos nodded slowly.

"Never knew who he was, where he came form or where he went. He was an old Indian that came walking out of the hills one day and asked my father for some food. Dad took a liking to the old man and let him stay. We found out later that he was the one that told Randolph the secret of the creature and how to catch him. I saw the old one once or twice, as I said, I was ten when it happened.

Randolph had wanted his father to have some happiness and had urged him to remarry. In 1927, my father had married Grace Villanueva, the daughter of the, then, county sheriff. I was born the following year. Due to the great age difference between my father and me, Randolph was more like my father than my brother.

The old one told my brother something that excited him. I know that he had planned something for that Halloween; he had recruited several of the younger vaqueros to go with him and had something that he referred to as a secret weapon.

They were armed as if for a small war. That day, he and his men were ready to ride out when word came that there was a problem at the Fuentes Ranch. Randolph was engaged to Grace Fuentes.

Randolph was a natural born leader. I tried to follow, but he refused to allow me to come with him when there was danger. This probably saved my life. He gathered as many armed men as he could and raced across the valley to the Fuentes Ranch. I heard my father talk to the survivors.

They arrived to find the hacienda in flames. Don Rafael Fuentes and his men were staging a last stand in the center of the courtyard.

Massive creatures were wading among them, killing everything in sight. The weapons of the defenders seemed to have little effect on the creatures.

According to the few survivors, Randolph and his men hit the creatures in the rear like the wrath of God. For some reason, even though the weapons of Don Rafael and his men had little effect on those things; the bullets fired by Randolph and his men had a drastic impact. They killed several of the creatures. Then Randolph saw something huge drop from the skies and grab his fiancée in its claws.

Randolph sprang from his horse and dropped on top of the creature. He pulled his knife and rammed it into the creature time after time. He actually forced the thing to its knees, if that thing had knees. Dropping Grace Fuentes, the thing turned its attention to Randolph and tried to shake him off. He refused to release his hold. It finally grabbed the woman again, spread its wings and, with Randolph still cutting at it with his knife, flew into the night.

No one ever saw my brother or his woman again. Losing Randolph almost killed my father. I cursed God that night that I wasn't with Randolph to help him."

"Mr. Santos, I am sorry to put you through this, I didn't know."

He looked at her and smiled a surprisingly gentle smile.

"No reason you should have known, my dear. I am one of the few who are left that remember that Halloween Night, so long ago. I outlived my usefulness to anyone long ago. I have only my memories of a happier time left."

"You friend is ready to go." interrupted a soft voice.

Sheila looked up to see Ringo looking at her through the doorway. Santos stood and took her arm.

"Come, my dear," he said gently, "It's time for you to go. Leave me with my memories."

For a long moment the two stood and locked eyes. Something about the old man seemed to stir some faint memories in the far recesses of his mind.

"Black one ready to pay," interrupted Ringo, "Me go back to fire."

With that, Ringo turned and shuffled back toward the other door that led to the back.

"Crazy old coot." snorted Santos as he led Sheila out to get his money from the customer, "Don't know why I let him stay here, anyways. He's nothing but a royal pain in the keister."

Walking over to the counter, Santos searched his pockets for a stub of a pencil. Then his tongue clenched between his yellow teeth, Santos painfully and slowly figured up the bill for the things that the Black Robe had ordered. When he finished his math, Santos slowly rechecked his figures. Finally satisfied with his math, Santos pushed the paper across the counter toward his customer.

"Comes to one hundred and thirty dollars; cash money. Check fer yourself if'n you don't believe me."

Wordlessly, the Black Robe pulled a roll of bills from a hidden pocket and counted out the amount requested. The remaining money was returned to the same hidden pocket and then the robed one pointed in the general direction of the old Mission.

"What? Oh, you want me to have them delivered?"

Another nod was the only answer he received.

"Well, sure, I guess. I mean, I'll be happy to have old Ringo bring them up to you. But I can't till this wind dies down tomorrow. Why, this here wind would blow that scrawny old Injun plumb away." Santos laughed, slapping the counter with the flat of his hand.

"My sister?" questioned Sheila.

Santos bit his lip for a moment and then reluctantly nodded.

"Woman, you is hard to say no to. Sure, when she gets here I'll help her get up to the Old Mission."

Impulsively, Sheila leaned over and kissed one of his weather beaten cheeks; her soft lips bringing a smile to the old man's face.

With a shrug, the Black Robe gathered up the various bags containing his purchases in his arms, glided across the floor, and out into the storm, the door closing softly behind him. Sheila grabbed the few that the Black robe had missed and strode after him. Santos watched them go, then suddenly darted to the door and peered out the window, following his customers' path with his eyes. A few steps down the street sat an old green pickup truck. Struggling against the high wind, Sheila forced open the passenger door as the Black Robe pulled open the driver's side door. They dumped the bags inside, and then the Black robe climbed in behind the wheel. The engine started and the old truck clattered down the street.

"Darn," muttered the old man, turning from the window, "Still didn't see nothing. One day, I'll get a glimpse of one o'them critters."

Seeing nothing else of interest in sight, Santos stomped across the store and entered the small office again. Talking to Sheila had revived old memories that he had long thought forgotten. The pain of loss he had felt at the death of Randolph was still as fresh as the day it happened. He felt the need to do something, but had no idea what he could do. With a start he realized that the next day would make it exactly sixty years ago that Randolph had died.

His old eyes narrowing, he considered the old stories he had heard. If the old legends were true, then the next night, the creature would walk again. This time, he'd be ready. First he rummaged in his battered old desk and found the old .44 that his daddy had given him. Randolph's gun, found trampled in the dirt where it had fallen in his battle with the winged creature. He pulled papers out of another drawer until he found a box of ammunition that fit the old gun.

Glancing at the clock, he noticed that it was time for the news, he reaching over and turned the radio to his favorite channel as he fondly rubbed the smooth grip of the old gun. It was probably his imagination, but just handling the old weapon made him feel closer to his dead brother.

"Continuing the news, the top story is the unusual weather that is plaguing southern New Mexico and West Texas. The unusual weather patterns have caused massive flooding that has forced the closing of parts of Interstate 10 and Interstate 25.

According to the weather service, the wind will reach gusts of up to one hundred and forty miles per hour between now and midnight, but will die down to normal levels by dawn tomorrow. The rain will taper off by midnight tonight. Stay tuned for further broadcasts."

Santos nodded his head and muttered to himself.

"I knowed it! I knowed it!" Santos mumbled to himself. "This ain't no storm to worry about. The wind has to blow for several days before that old haint walks. Everbody's worried fer nothing."

"Voice in box wrong," came a deep voice from behind him.

Santos spun around in his chair with a start, the old pistol falling from his hand to clatter on the scarred hard wood floor. Old Ringo stood framed in the doorway.

"What's that you say you old heathen!" snapped Santos, leaning over to grope at his feet for the pistol. "You really been running your mouth tonight."

Ringo ignored Santos' question, turning and walking back to the living quarters where Santos allowed Ringo to sleep near the fire. Sitting and staring at the old gun for a few minutes, Santos finally got to his feet and followed the old Indian back to the kitchen. He went directly to the stove and poured himself a mug of hot coffee. As he got older, he was sure that the cold penetrated his house easier. Ringo sat hunched over, by the fire, nursing his own cup of coffee.

"Well, this here storm'll be over tonight. Won't be no haints bothering us this night." cackled Santos.

"Not true." rumbled Ringo, never raising his eyes from his cup, "This major bad storm. Last all week. Evil one will walk tonight, tomorrow night and maybe every night."

Santos snorted as he poured cream and sugar into his own cup.

"What do you mean, you old fool? Didn't you hear what the radio said? Wind stops tomorrow, rain stops at midnight, tonight."

Ringo shrugged, "You say. Me say that Radioman wrong. This storm is not natural, but the work of the evil one. He will walk tonight. He will kill tonight. He has already killed this night."

Santos turned and glared at the old Indian.

"Sometimes I think you're plumb crazy old man. What makes you think that this here storm won't end just like they said on the radio?"

Ringo sat silently sipping his coffee for a long time, and then he raised his head and looked at Santos.

"Fred Santos, you and your family has been good to me over the years. I have no wish to see you harmed. I have lived long, longer than the Great Spirit normally allows and seen much in those many years. I know things about this land that the white man has never seen. This is an evil land; it has always been an evil land. It was used as a prison by the Great Spirit for things that should never have lived.

Neither my people nor any of their cousins would set foot in valley even during the worst of times. When snows would come so deep that my people froze to death in their lodges, this valley would be warm. Even then, none of my people would come, even to save their lives.

At certain times, the walls of this prison created by the Great Spirit get thin and must be renewed. Only blood can renew the walls, blood and sacrifice. The evil one is here, I can feel his presence. He wakens in his eternal prison and wants to once again walk the earth.

Also, I feel something else--- there is another who comes to this place. One who is like no other. Him the evil one fears. Unless something happens to change it, this place will be a battleground for creatures with powers you and yours cannot imagine."

Santos walked over to the sink, peering out the window. He had to admit that the storm showed no sign of ending, but them scientific fellers knew all about this stuff. He had once heard a radio show about weather forecasting. Those folks could tell you a month in advance when it would rain. With a sniff he threw the rest of his coffee into the sink.

"Ah, you're just a crazy old Indian. You don't know shit. Them radio fellers, now they got ways of telling all about the weather. This time tomorrow, you'll be back in your garden out there praying to your heathen gods to send rain to your damn tomatoes."

He swung around ready to defend his position, but Ringo had gone back to starring in his cup. Not another word did the old Indian say for several hours.

Finally tiring of Ringo's silence and a little unnerved if he had to admit it. Old Fred Santos went back to his office and rummaged around until he found his brother's old cartridge belt. The old .44 slid smoothly into the battered holster. Standing, he struggled until he could fasten the old belt around his thick waist. He'd show that old haint a thing or two if he came into Seven Brother's Trading Post. He'd do what Randolph and Ben had failed to do. He'd kill that damn thing. He sat back in his chair and thought for a second, then snapped his fingers. He needed help; he'd call his old partner Dusty.

Swiveling his chair to the left, Santos picked up the phone and carefully punched out Dusty's number. Just as he heard his old friend answer in his gravelly voice, the phone went dead and the power went out. Sitting in the dark, the only sound that old Fred Santos could hear was the howling of the wind and the beat of the sand and rain against the windows. There was a peculiar sound in the darkness of the store.

Fred Santos rose to his booted feet and backed against the inner wall of his office, pulling his pistol. With a start he realized that he hadn't loaded the thing. With a feeling of disgust, he tightened his grip on his old pistol and groped on the desk for the ammunition. Suddenly, he heard a sound outside his office door. He felt a tremor of fear.

"Wh----Who's there?" he croaked, "one move and I'll blast you where you stand."

"Not with an empty gun, my friend. It is I," rumbled a deep voice that he recognized as being similar to the voice of old Ringo, "The evil one has many helpers. They are on their way to this town. The conflict has begun. The Other will also be here soon. By tonight, all the players in this age-old game will be in place.

"Stay out of what happens, my old friend, or you will surely die. Let the game play itself out as the Great Spirit meant for it to happen. You still blame yourself for not dying with Randolph or with Ben when they faced the evil one. But you could have done nothing. Only the Other has even a small chance of defeating the evil one, if he will."

Santos literally jumped across the little office and rushed through the doorway into the store. He was going to give that Indian a piece of his mind.

"Damn it, old man! What the bloody hells are you talking about? Who's the Other?" he demanded waving his unloaded pistol about the dark room. His anger vanished when he discovered that the store was deserted. He was sure that Ringo had spoken from just outside his office door, but the old Indian was not there.

Muttering to himself, Santos felt his way across the store, headed for Ringo's favorite spot beside the big fireplace in the kitchen.

"Ringo, you old heathen, where are you? What the hell were you talking about? Who's this Other?"

He stepped into the old kitchen and stopped, glaring his anger. The light from the fireplace showed that the kitchen was empty.

"Ringo, you answer me you old faker!"

Receiving no answer, Santos stomped across to the fireplace, but Ringo was not sitting motionless in the deep shadows, as was his custom. The flickering firelight gave enough light for Ringo to tell that the kitchen was empty except for him. The old Indian was gone.

"Fred Santos," came the whispery voice from behind him.

Santos spun around to see the shadowy figure in the doorway he had just come through. He was sure that he hadn't walked past anyone when he has entered the room. Santos squinted trying to identify who it was.

"Ringo, that you?" he demanded, lifting the empty pistol as if it could protect him.

"That is the name by which you knew me, my old friend," said the oddly sounding voice. "It is as Ringo that I have lived for so many years to obey the command of the Great Spirit."

Santos cocked his head to one side and took a step toward the figure.

"What the hell are you talking about, you silly old man!"

Santos heard a deep sigh from the shadowy figure before him.

"Stay back, my friend. I have lived all my life hoping that this day would never come. I have come to like and respect you and your family, Fred Santos. I loved your brother Randolph as the son I never had, but the evil one was not to be denied. I have some affection for this town, so I have no wish to see it harmed."

"You knew Randolph?" asked Santos in a stunned voice.

"I am the one you know as the Old One. I believed that Randolph was the successor to the Other, but that was not to be. I tried to arm him for a battle I had no wish for him to fight, but he would not be denied.

"Unfortunately, I had no control over what happened then, nor do I have any control over what will happen now. The imprisoned one will break loose. The walls of his prison have grown too thin, as the Great Spirit has, in truth, also weakened as his children have turned away from him.

"Now, nothing can stop the Prince of Evil from once again walking the earth. Maybe the Other can put him back in his prison and maybe he cannot. Either way, a battle will rage in this place unlike any you have ever seen. I am old, my friend, older than you can even begin to imagine. I have stayed here to try and protect those that I could. Now the time has come when my protection is not enough. I must go to meet the Other. Take care, my old friend."

Where there had been shadow and whispers, Santos could see a faint glow that gradually became brighter. At the center of the light was old Ringo, but he was no longer the old man that Santos had known for so many years. Instead of his wrinkled, stooped old friend, there stood a tall, strongly built, Indian Warrior of middle years. A beautiful bonnet of eagle feathers crowned his long black hair. In his left hand was a weapon unlike any that Santos had ever seen. Raising one hand in farewell, Ringo slowly faded from sight.

Fred Santos stood alone in his fire lit kitchen. Alone. Outside the storm raged uncontrollably.

CHAPTER FOURTEEN

The interstate highway between Albuquerque, New Mexico and El Paso, Texas is a long straight trip down Interstate 25 to Interstate 10. There are only one or two small towns and one almost city to break the monotony. Normally, the trip is boring, but an easy drive, with little traffic. However, on this dreary stormy day, the Santa Ana winds were blowing from the west, bringing with them sheets of fine gritty sand. When the hot Santa Ana wind blows, only those with pressing business normally take to the highways in Southern New Mexico.

With nothing to block it path, the winds blow across the flat terrain with gale force. There are times that the wind can reach such levels that vehicles can be over turned and send tumbling across the dunes. To travel in such high winds was to take one's life in their hands.

On this windy Monday morning, the only car on the highway for miles was a prison transfer van from Central Prison in Santa Fe, New Mexico. Inside the van was F.B.I. Special Agent in Charge, Allen Spector, of the El Paso F.B.I. Office, Corrections Officer and driver, Marty Kramer and two very special prisoners. Mason (Mace) Runnels, a former assassin for a Mexican drug cartel that had gone one a killing spree in southern New Mexico until apprehended by Spector, himself, and another prisoner known only as Number 35.

Mason (Mace) Runnels was of medium height and didn't weigh over a hundred and fifty pounds. He was so average in appearance that he tended to blend in with any crowd, a skill that made him a very effective assassin. He was also a very deadly martial artist, able kill with his bare hands. In the prison hierarchy, Mace Runnels was given a great deal of respect.

His seatmate and fellow prisoner was a big man, standing over six feet three inches tall in his bare feet. Deceptively thin, no one would be able to guess the almost superhuman strength possessed by the big man. Though ruggedly handsome and friendly looking, no one knew anything about Number 35. As far as anyone knew, Number 35 had been found during a prison excavation and identified as a dead prisoner from years back, in fact, only as far by going as far back in the archives as the records of Central went, had records of prisoner Number 35 being incarcerated at that facility been. Though he looked no older than his mid-thirties, based on the records, he had to be at least eighty years old. As usual, he had spoken not a word since the trip began. It was a mystery that the FBI wanted to examine at a more sophisticated facility.

Kramer was bored; he had made this trip at least a hundred times, running prisoners and V.I.P.s to and from El Paso. The only thing that made this trip any different was the lousy weather. Out of boredom more than any interest, Kramer tried to start a conversation.

"Hey Agent Spector, why are we taking these two over to El Paso? What's so special about them?"

Spector glanced back at the two, handcuffed to the rear seat. Runnels gave him a bright smile, while Number 35 just sat quietly, staring straight ahead. As always, his expression was totally blank.

"Well, Mr. Runnels is needed for a grand jury investigation into cross border drug traffic. My team of agents will take charge of him when we arrive at the El Paso jail and formally transfer him into federal custody."

Kramer smirked and glanced into the rear view mirror, meeting Runnels' eyes.

"Getting new digs, are we Runnels?"

Runnels smiled his bright smile, but Spector noticed that his eyes were cold, like a cobra's.

"Seems so, Mr. Kramer. Be sorry to leave my humble home, but we each have to do what we have to do."

Kramer glanced back at the road as an unusually forceful gust of wind threatened to cause him to lose control.

"Well, why take Number 35, he doesn't know anything about anything, does he? I've been at the prison for three years and he hasn't caused one minutes of trouble in that entire time. In fact, I don't think he's said three words in the entire three years that I have been a guard."

Agent Spector shrugged, his hands nervously griping the dash as he braced himself against the jerking of the van, "Well, primarily because he's a real puzzle. It seems that there are no records of his arrest, trial, conviction or sentence. In fact there are no records of him at all. His prints are not in any database possessed by any agency. In spite of that, he was found in the excavation for the new expansion and it was found that he matches the description of a prisoner from the early part of this century. He's being transferred into federal custody so that a final disposition can be made of his case."

Kramer nodded, turning his attention back to the road. Though he would not admit it, the weather really had him somewhat worried. He was seriously worried when it began to rain again. The water was coming down in such solid sheets that the van was periodically sliding on the water-covered pavement.

"Well, Agent Spector, I'm here to tell you that it's getting hard to keep this bucket of bolts on this highway. The cross winds are too strong and change direction often enough that it's hard for me to keep control. We may have to find a place to pull off and wait out the storm."

Spector nodded, turning back again to check his prisoners.

"You're the driver, Kramer, if you think we can't make it then we'll stop. My only question is where we can stop that'll get us out of the weather. I don't remember anything close to the Interstate between here and Truth or Consequences."

Kramer took one hand from wrestling with the wheel, pointing toward the glove compartment.

"There's a map of the area in there. Find us a small town where we can wait it out. There are several in these hills to our south and west. Just tell me which exit to take. I'll get us there."

Spector pulled a map out of the glove box and flipped on the map light in the center console. Carefully he studied the map, finally finding what he was looking for. With his finger marking the spot he leaned over to show the driver his proposed destination. Suddenly something crashed into the back of his head, knocking him forward. Agent Spector fell from his seat and slumped in the floor, out cold.

Kramer glanced in his rear view mirror and saw Runnels removing his handcuffs. Number 35 still sat, staring straight ahead.

"I wondered when you was going to make your move, Runnels," he said as he continued to struggle with the wheel.

Runnels leaned over the seat to peer out the window at the rain.

"Timing is everything," he said as he slid his hands into Spector's coat and removed the agent's pistol and identification. "Where are we?"

Kramer motioned toward the passenger seat.

"There's a map. We're getting off at the next exit and taking the old back roads working our way to an old town called El Noche. That's where your people are gonna meet us and I'll get paid."

Runnels nodded absently as he studied the map.

"How far's the exit you mean to take?"

"Just up ahead," answered Kramer, straining to keep the van on the highway. The wind continually threatened to blow them sideways.

Kramer suddenly braked to ease the van through a small lake that covered the Interstate Highway. Just beyond the watery roadblock was the exit they meant to take, blocked by a few wind blown items that were easily circumvented. With a surge of power, the van roared up the exit ramp, to slide to a stop at the intersection. There was no other traffic insight.

"Hold it a minute, pull over to the side of the road just ahead," ordered Runnels.

Kramer slowed where Runnels had indicated and allowed the engine to idle. Runnels leaned over the seat and muscled opened the passenger door. He placed the pistol against Spector's head, pulled back the hammer and pulled the trigger. Blood splattered the interior of the passenger door.

Kramer jumped and turned pale.

"Jesus, what was that for?"

With a grunt, Runnels pushed the dead Agent's body out the door, and then climbed over the seat to sit comfortably in the passenger seat. He pulled the rear view mirror over to critically examine his appearance. Carefully, he smoothed his windblown hair back into place.

"I don't like feds," he explained in a bland voice, "and I don't like this fed in particular. He's the one that caught me. Even worse, he embarrassed me with the ease with which he caught me. I swore when I got sent up that I'd get him. Now I got him."

"Man, I didn't make no agreement to commit no murder. It was a straight deal to simply help you escape and your people would pay me one million dollars in cash. Not one word was said about killing nobody," snarled Kramer. "Hell do you have any idea what would happen to me if we get caught. Me, a guard and everything, hell, they'd give me the chair just for helping you escape."

It was finally dawning on him that taking part in this little venture to help Runnels escape was not as simple as he had believed. Win, lose or draw, it would make him an outcast for life. The picture of Spector's shattered head kept coming back before his eyes. At this moment, a million dollars didn't look so great. If they got caught before he could get across the border with his money, he would face prison just like Runnels. Former Corrections Officer didn't live long on the other side of the bars.

Runnels twirled Spector's pistol around his trigger finger, whistling a merry little tune. Suddenly Kramer found himself looking down the barrel of the little pistol; Runnels' cold eyes studied him, unblinking.

"You don't tell me what to do, Kramer! Nobody tells me what to do. You're being well paid to help me escape. Fine, then help me to escape, get me to El Noche. Otherwise, keep your comments to yourself or you can join your friend on the side of the road." snarled the former prisoner.

Kramer took a slow breath, his eyes riveted on the pistol facing him. He realized that death was just a finger twitch away at this moment.

"Sure---Sure Runnels. Whatever you say, man. Just take it easy, I'll get you there and then you can take off with your friends."

"How far's the border?" Runnels asked, his demeanor changing again, the usual smile covering his face as he began twirling the revolver around his trigger finger again.

"Bout sixty miles or so. You should be in Mexico about two and a half hours after your guys pick you up. After they pay me my million dollars, that is."

Runnels smiled his cobra smile, glancing at the driver out of the corner of one eye.

"Don't worry, Marty, me boy, you'll be well taken care of. You're worth every dime of the million they promised. You did your job."

Kramer grinned widely; he could picture that million dollars now. He only had to deliver Runnels to that old ghost town and pick up his money. He'd retire and live in one of them Mexican Resorts.

Number 35 still sat silently, staring out at the rain. His dark eyes fixed on a future his companions could not see. Only his slowly steady breathing indicated that he was alive.

CHAPTER FIFTEEN

Outside traffic stopping in the center of El Noche was a rare event. The town was on few maps and actually consisted of no more than two parallel streets, one on either side of a town square. Of the two dozen or more buildings, some dating back to the mid-1800s that made up the town only those immediately adjoining the square were occupied. So isolated was the old town that those who lived in El Noche Valley seldom saw anyone but their neighbors.

So, while there was no one outside in the ever-increasing storm, word spread quickly around town regarding the limo with New York plates that was sitting at the edge of the town square. Several residents had remarked on the fact that the car had circled the town at least a half a dozen times before stopping to idle near the old church.

"Of all the places to pick to meet Mace, why did they have to pick this wide spot in the road?" demanded the driver, Nick "Fingers" Martony, as he surveyed the deserted streets of El Noche. "Nothing here but rain and sand. I don't see a single soul. You sure this is the place, boss?"

The man he addressed as his boss, Carlos Molena, of one of the New York crime families, leaned forward to look over the seat and peer out the front window. Though he wouldn't admit it even to someone as close to him as Fingers, he was also having second thoughts about the entire situation. His nerves were on edge for some reason.

"Nick, you're a worrier. This place is perfect for our purposes. It's close to the Interstate, but relatively isolated. It's only a little over fifty miles to the Mexican border. Hell, there aren't but five hundred people within twenty miles of this place. We can't very well pick up an obvious escaped prisoner on the main street of a bustling community, now can we?"

He leaned back in his seat and crossed his legs.

"Besides, the weather will make it harder to track the van when the cops discover that it's been hijacked. He gets here; we get in the car and simply drive off. Neat and clean."

Molena paused as a chill ran down his back. He couldn't shake the feeling that something was definitely wrong about this place. In fact, he hadn't liked being part of this entire operation from the beginning. Runnels was a loose cannon that could go off at any time, but he knew too much that, if revealed to the cops, could make a lot of highly placed people on both sides of the law very uncomfortable.

Sitting back, he instinctively glanced to his left to confirm that his personal bodyguard, Tiny Joe, was sitting in his accustomed place against the left passenger door. With Tiny Joe's six feet nine inches, four hundred pounds of muscle between him and the world, Carlos Molena had survived the fiercest of the New York underworld gang wars. Molena went nowhere without Tiny Joe.

Reassured, he leaned forward and tapped Fingers on the right shoulder.

"Tell you what Nick, we got a while to wait, so find some place in this burg where we can get a cup of coffee or something to eat. I'm hungry."

"Sure, Boss." Martony said as he glanced around the wind swept square. The driver peered in every direction but didn't even see a light burning in any of the buildings around the square. Visibility was limited due to the rapidly fading light and the driving rain; it appeared to the New Yorker that the town was totally deserted.

Martony glanced at his watch and noticed that it was only 4:30 p.m., much too early for the stores to be closed. Then he noticed that there were no streetlights. As a boy raised in Brooklyn, he was used to streetlights. There were none here. He found the situation totally puzzling, it was much too dark for 4:30, perhaps his watch had stopped.

"Hey, Boss, what time you got?"

Molena flipped on one of the backseat courtesy lights and checked his expensive Rolex.

"About 4:30, Nick. Why, what's the problem? Gonna catch a train?" laughed his boss.

Nick waved toward the outside. "You ever seen it this dark at 4:30 in the afternoon? I tell you something about this place just ain't right. I don't like it here."

Molena shook his head, sorry that his old friend was losing his nerve.

"Nick, it's fine. Just find us a place to eat and everything will be fine."

That request was much easier said than done. Nick cruised slowly around the town and didn't see a single place open, much less one that served food. Just as Nick was ready to give up, he noticed the gleam of light coming from one of the buildings on the square to his right front. He couldn't tell what type of business might be located there, but it was the only light that he had spotted since they had arrived in this ghost town. Anything was better than sitting in the freezing car.

Slipping the car into drive, Martony pulled the limo up in front of the building and noticed a faded sigh that proclaimed the building "Mabel's Cafe". There were thick wooden shutters over the windows and the door was firmly shut against the elements. Even though Martony had seen a light, there was no sign of life.

"Looks like we might be able to get some food here, boss." said Martony over his shoulder. "I'm sure that I saw a light coming from this place."

Molena cranked his window down a bit and glanced at the building Martony indicated.

"Looks closed to me, Nick," said Molena dubiously.

Nick shook his head, "No, it's gotta be open, boss. I know that I saw a light this building just a few seconds ago."

"Well, you saw the light, so get your ass out there and make sure," ordered Molena. "I don't want to get my new suit dirty if the place is closed."

Muttering to himself, Martony shouldered open the car door and jumped out, the wind tearing his new hat away from him before he had gone two steps. Swearing in two languages, Martony made a useless grab for his hat as it sailed of for pats unknown, then turned and ran up the steps to grab the doorknob. The door flew open almost at the same moment he touched it and he almost fell inside the dimly lit cafe. Sitting around three tables lit by a couple of small oil lamps were about a half a dozen people, all of whom were looking curiously at Nick. Nearby a small fire crackled merrily in an ornate, brick fireplace.

Martony and the man who had opened the door for him both fought the power of the wind to close the door. Martony finally had to use his shoulder and all of his strength to literally force the door shut against the wind.

"Howdy, stranger." said one old man at a nearby table, once the door was safely closed and the roaring sound of the wind was partially shut out.

Nick nodded suspiciously, accepting a bar towel to wipe off the worst of the water, as his eyes scanned the place. He wanted to make sure that there were no cops in the room.

"You still serving food?" asked Nick, tossing the now soaking wet towel on the bar.

A big man wearing a dirty apron and slowly wiping his hands on a rag, came out from behind the counter and shook his head.

"Fraid I can't offer nothing but coffee and booze, stranger. Well actually, maybe I could rustle up a cold sandwich or two." commented the big man, "All the electric power in town went out about an hour ago. My cooking stove is all electrical. Everything went at the same time. Hell, even my thermostat don't work for the gas heat."

He stopped for a moment and motioned at around the room.

"Luckily we always keep these old oil lamps around. These here lamps and that fireplace over yonder is all the light and heat we got. Grab a table and join us as we sit out this storm. If you want, I can get you a cup of coffee. Got a little gas operated camping stove to keep the coffee at least warm."

Martony glanced around the room. He didn't see anyone or anything that could endanger his boss, finally he nodded.

"Sure, make it three cups of coffee. I'll get my associates from the car."

Pulling his coat collar up Martony wrenched open the door, almost being blown from his feet by the wind that came through the open door. Bent over, he ran out the door and back down the steps. Temporarily sheltered from the wind by the bulk of the car, he pulled open the right rear door and stuck his head inside the car.

"Boss, this building is a café, but the power's out around here. That's why the whole town is darker than pitch. There's just a bunch of old geezers sitting around in the dark drinking coffee. We'd probably be better in some place like this than sitting out here in the open. Come on inside."

Molena sat and thought for a minute then nodded.

"Well, we gotta wait for Mace to get here and with this wind, there's no telling when, or even if, he'll be able to get here. We may as well join the locals. That'll be better than freezing our butts off in this damn cold car. Let's go."

Martony moved aside and helped Molena out of the car. Tiny Joe exited the other side of the car, showing no more sign of strain than he would in opening the car door on a warm summer day. The force of the high winds seemed not to bother the monster.

Slamming the door, the Martony and Molena made a mad dash up the steps. Tiny Joe came slowly behind them, his piggy eyes taking in everything. His job was to protect Mr. Molena and he had killed more than one man with his bare hands to carry out his job. The big cook held the door open for them as the three came inside; the two smaller men shaking water from their sodden suit coats.

The cook struggled against the force of the wind to close the door, but was having no luck. The force of the wind was getting stronger by the moment. Martony went to help the cook, but not even the two of them could force the door completely shut. Molena glanced at Tiny Joe and motioned toward the door. Lumbering over, the giant placed one hand on the door, moved the other two back, and gave what appeared to be a gentle push. The door slammed shut. The cook's eyes bulged in amazement.

"Man, you're some kind of strong."

Tiny Joe just gave a nod and walked over to stand behind Molena.

"Is it always like this?" asked Molena, squeezing the water from his longish hair to fall in a puddle at his feet. "I'm soaked clear through."

"Well, sonny," responded one of the old men at a nearby table, "We've had storms before, but nothing like this. Come on over by the fire and dry out."

Grateful for the offer, Molena shrugged of his soaking wet jacket and hung it on a chair by the fire. He moved over and stood with his back to the fire and began to relax as he felt the warmth begin to spread through him. He actually started to doze on his feet until Nick brought him a cup of hot coffee.

"Where you boys from?" asked one of the older women sitting nearby.

"New York City. We're down here on business, got lost in this storm." answered Molena. Nick left all the talking up to his boss, sitting quietly with his back to the wall, watching for potential trouble. Tiny Joe took up his place near the chimney, out of the way, yet close to Molena.

Suddenly the front door slammed back against the wall as a raincoat-covered figure came stumbling inside, propelled by the force wind. The cook ran over to help the new comer wrestle the door shut. This time, the two were able to get the door firmly shut, before the new comer removed his coat. Nick went on full alert when the firelight reflected off the badge on the newcomer's chest. Tiny Joe shifted his position to edge closer to Molena. The new customer was the county sheriff.

"God, it's wet outside," said the newcomer as he tossed his raincoat toward the coat rack and crowded close to the fire, to stand by Molena. "How about some of that hot coffee of yours, Petey?"

"Coming up, Sheriff." responded the big cook, coming around the counter with a big steaming mug.

Cupping the hot cup in his big hands for warmth, the Sheriff came over to stand by the fire. It was obvious that he was soaked to the skin.

"How's road conditions, Sheriff?" asked Petey, going over to look through a crack in the wooden shutters.

The Sheriff took a long drink of the hot coffee in his hands before shaking his head.

"Not good, I'm afraid." he said, backing closer to the fire. "The old bridge on the south road's been washed away. The arroyos are beginning to flood and the water had washed away some power poles. Really the only way out of the valley is the old county road back to Interstate 25. If that particular road is blocked, then we're sealed in this here valley until the bridge is repaired."

The lawman looked around and noticed Molena and Martony. His eyes widened slightly when he caught sight of the massive Tiny Joe lurking in the shadows. Keeping one eye on Tiny Joe, he turned and held out his hand toward Molena.

"Howdy, stranger, I'm Ben Stark, County Sheriff. If you don't mind my asking, which way did you men come in?"

"Jackson, Arnie Jackson." responded Molena. "As to how we got here, we came up from the south, from El Paso," added Molena, moving further back into the shadows beside the fireplace, getting closer to his bodyguard. "Bridge was fine when we came across. But, I will say that it was not raining near this hard when we got here."

Stark finished his cup and held it out toward Petey for a refill.

"Well, you're sure a lucky so and so. That old bridge must have let go just after you crossed. County has been trying to raise the money to replace it for years, but there's not that many people in the county."

Taking his cup back from the cook, the Sheriff took a long sip and sighed deeply.

"At the moment, I'm afraid that you're stuck here with the rest of us until I can find out about the road to the west. I was really serious about that being the only way out of the valley if the bridge is out."

Molena looked uneasily at Nick, but Nick was so far back in the shadows that he was only a darker spot in the deep shadows. Their plans for getting Mace out of the area definitely did not call for going any further west.

"Well, we're only here for a little coffee and then we're planning on going on to the Interstate." began Molena. "My driver is an expert, I'm sure that we'll be fine, Sheriff."

Stark frowned at Molena and glanced toward where Nick sat.

"Well, Mr. Jackson, I really don't care how expert your driver is. If there's been a landslide on Devil's Hill all the expert driving in the world ain't going to save you. The road to the north cuts through the edge of Devil's Hill.

That being the case, I'm afraid that I can't let you boys leave here just yet. It just ain't safe."

Molena started to argue, but then was hit by an idea. He could tell that Nick and Tiny Joe were just waiting for the word and Sheriff Ben Stark was history. At the same time, he couldn't control the entire population of this little burg with just two guys. No he had to play it smart.

"Well, if you say so Sheriff, then I guess we'll just sit here for a while longer. At least as long as the coffee holds out. Guess I'll just sit over here and dry out." he said walking over to drop into a chair at the table that Nick has chosen against the wall.

Stark finished the second cup of coffee and sat the cup on the edge of a nearby table. Walking over to the hat rack, he starting putting his raincoat back on.

"Well, I'm going back to watch the Devil's Hill cut. The arroyos around that area are filling fast and starting to undermine the road itself. If that road goes, then we're in deep shit; there'll be four feet of water in the streets before midnight. You all take care and I'll see you in a while."

"Let me get that door for you, Ben." offered Petey walking over to unlatch the outer door. However, when the cook pulled open the door, a small figure came charging in, actually the small figure was almost thrown into the room, to be caught in the sheriff's big hands.

The rest of the customers in the café watched in surprise as the bundled up figure began to babble and wave its arms at the Sheriff. Sheriff Stark drew back one of his big hands and slapped the figure across the face. The babbling stopped in mid word.

"Now that we've got that over with, what the problem, Benji?" asked Stark guiding the slight figure to a chair near the fire.

Pulling the big hat from his head, the figure was revealed to be a rather small young man, his clothing torn and muddy, his hair disheveled, a wild look on his youthful features. Stark bent down on one knee, bringing his eyes on the level of the youngster.

"Now, Benji, what's the problem?"

"Sheriff, it was awful. It was terrible, I mean, nothing was left. All dead." he babbled, his eyes wild.

"Benji, if you don't slow down and tell me what's wrong, then I can't help you, can I?" soothed the Sheriff.

With a visible effort, the young man stopped shivering and fixed his wild eyes on the Sheriff's harsh features.

"It's Uncle Zeke, Sheriff. I went out there this morning, but he wasn't in the house. I waited and waited, but finally went to look for him. I thought he might be out with the cows so I went to the cow pen behind the barn."

The young man paused, his face white as a sheet. His fingers worked, grabbing nothing but air.

"Go on, son." urged the Sheriff, placing one of his large hands on the boy's shoulder. "What'd you find?"

"The cows, they were all dead. There was forty or more of them. There was blood all over the place."

His taciturn features hidden in the flickering shadows, the Sheriff stayed motionless. His eyes bored into that of the youth.

"Any idea what killed the cattle?" asked the lawman.

Shakily, the youth nodded.

"They were ripped to pieces. There were cow parts scattered all over the area. There was blood everywhere."

"Any tracks?"

Benji shivered again.

"Couldn't tell with all the mud and rain."

"Any sign of that Uncle of yours?" asked Mrs. Minnie Foster, coming over to place an arm around the boy's shoulders.

Not taking his eyes off the Sheriff, the youth nodded slowly.

"Oh, I saw him, all right. I didn't see him at first, just the blood all over everything and all the dead cows. I knew that I should do something, but I didn't do anything, I just froze, I didn't know what to do. It was so spooky in the darkness, with the wind howling like it was. It wasn't until I went back around to the front of the barn that I found Uncle Zeke. He was in lying in the mud in front of the barn. He---he was covered with blood. His eyes were open, staring up at me as if he was watching me. But he was dead, I just knew he was dead."

"Any idea what killed him?" asked the Sheriff.

"No," quavered the youth, tears beginning to stream down his face. "but the front of the barn was knocked out and his new bull was gone."

"Bet that new pet of his gored him," offered on of the old men.

"It's October 31st," responded Petey.

"Knock that shit off, Petey. That's an old wives tale," snapped Stark.

Getting to his feet, the Sheriff glanced at Mrs. Foster.

"Miss Minnie, can you take care of him. I'm going out to Zeke's place."

The youth quickly stood and grabbed his hat.

"I'm going with you, Sheriff. He's my only relative. I got a right."

Stark looked at him for a long moment, then nodded slowly.

"O.K. boy. But you stay close to me if anything happens."

Slapping his hat on his still damp hair, Ben nodded at Petey who opened the door. Stark lowered his head and literally fought his way across the wide porch against the heavy wind, the boy close behind him. As quickly as possible, they ran down the steps and jumped into the patrol car parked nearby. Petey strained with all his might to force the door closed again.

"Damn!" exclaimed Petey leaning against the vibrating door, "I do believe the storm is getting worse. I've never seen the wind this bad."

"Well," growled Tom Randall, one of the old men, "sounds to me like we're going to be stuck here for a long while. To me that's as good a reason for getting drunk as any. Petey where's that liquor bottle you keep under the counter?"

In a sudden lull in the drumming of the rain and the shrieking of the wind Randall's ears perked as he heard a low murmuring. Twisting around in his chair, he saw that the murmuring was coming from Minnie Foster, in the flickering firelight; he saw that her lips were moving as if she was talking to herself.

"Minnie, what's gotten into you, girl? You taken to talking to yourself now?" queried Tom Randall, a smirk on his broad face.

Minnie Foster spoke in a hollow voice without bothering to look at the smirking rancher.

"Yes, I'm talking and you should be too, Tom Randall. I'm praying that we get through the night, that's what I'm doing."

Randall snorted in derision as he took the whiskey bottle offered by Petey.

"Praying?" he asked in surprise. "For what? Sure the storm's one of the worst that I've seen in many a year, but what's to pray about. We've got food, warmth and this old building is well over a hundred years old and solid as a rock. Ain't nothing to worry about."

"She's referring to the old stories about creatures that walk during the Santa Ana storms, Tom," answered Artie Prescott, the local mechanic.

At this Randall roared with laughter, slapping his thigh in amusement.

"Minnie Foster, I'm surprised at you!" he chortled, "Those old stories are nothing but legends. Monsters indeed! My pappy was telling me those stories fifty years ago. Weren't nothing to them then and there's nothing to them now. You must be getting senile."

Minnie Foster was a small woman, petite was the proper term. But in her anger, she seemed to grow before their eyes. She pointed her finger at Randall and spoke in a voice as hard as flint.

"Tom Randall, don't you scoff at what you don't understand. The monsters are real, I know, I have seen them slipping through the shadows: stalking the living. I've got the sight just as my mother and grandmother had. Those things are here haunting the valley as they have since the beginning of time."

Downing another shot of whiskey, Randall slammed his empty glass down on the table with enough force to make the bottle jump.

"You're losing it, Minnie. There ain't never been no monsters. Those old stories are just for scaring kids."

A hard smile crossed Minnie Foster's normally placid face.

"So they're just stores made up to scare the children? Tell that to my two poor cousins who worked for Don Raymond Santos and rode with Randolph that night sixty years ago. Tell that to Priscilla Fuentes, an orphan almost from birth after the creatures destroyed the Fuentes hacienda.

Go out to the ruins of the old Fuentes hacienda, which is haunted to this day by the souls of those poor people slaughtered by those godless creatures, and then tell me the stories are just made up to scare children. "

"Bah, old wives tales." said Randall, his attention full focused on his drinking, "That raid was done by Indians or Mexican raiders or some other natural explanation. There aren't and never were any monsters.

In my thirty years of ranching in this hellhole of a valley, I've not seen one single thing that would lead me to believe that any of these monsters actually exist. I, for one, don't believe in anything I can't see."

"What kind of monsters are you people talking about?" interrupted Carlos Molena.

"Legend and myth." snapped Randall, not even bothering to look at Molena.

"Ignore that old fool," returned Minnie Foster, her gaze back on the fire. "This valley has been haunted since before the coming of the red man by creatures that walk in darkness. Whenever the Santa Ana winds blow as they are now, the creatures come out and kill."

"What are Santa Ana winds?" asked Martony.

"The winds that are even now blowing." responded Minnie Foster, "The monsters are even now walking as they did when I was a girl."

"Crazy old bat!" offered Randall.

For a long moment, Foster was silent, and then she turned toward Randall.

"What do you think killed Zeke Marsters?"

Sheriff Ben Stark struggled to hold his patrol car on the muddy road as he headed for the Marsters' farm. Even though he was buckled securely in the passenger seat, Benji Marsters clutched the dash with his white knuckled hands.

"Not much further, Benji." said the Sheriff, as much to reassure himself as the boy, as he jerked the wheel to correct for a beginning skid.

Suddenly, his headlights picked out a figure standing on the side of the road as the Sheriff slammed on the brakes, fighting the wheel to stay on the road. Stopping with the patrol car sitting sideways in the road, the Sheriff forced open the door, flashlight in hand and slogged through the mud to the rear of the car. Benji came up to stand by him as the Sheriff methodically searched the side of the road with his powerful flashlight.

"What was it, Sheriff? What did you see?" demanded the boy, shading his eyes with his left hand, straining to see through the driving rain.

He knew he'd seen something standing by the road, but it was gone now. Seeing nothing, the Sheriff finally shook his head and turned back.

"Get back in the car, boy." He yelled. "You'll catch pneumonia in this rain."

Both back in the car, the Sheriff turned the defroster and the heater on high and held his frozen hands in front of the vents. Benji was scrunched down in the seat, huddled in his coat.

"What did you see?" he demanded.

"Well, boy, I—uh- well it looked like." he stammered, trying to get his thoughts in order.

"Like what?" prompted young Marsters.

"Boy you're gonna think I'm crazy, but it looked like a huge Indian, looked to be seven or eight feet tall."

"What's crazy about that, Sheriff?" questioned the boy, "there's Indians living hereabouts."

"Yeah, but this one had big horns growing out of his forehead."

CHAPTER SIXTEEN

"I don't know if I can keep this car on the highway much longer." complained Kramer, as he jerked the front wheels back on the pavement. Though they were partially sheltered by the steep hill to their left, the wind was tossing the van so badly that it felt like they were on a roller coaster.

"The wind's just too damn powerful, Runnels. Bigger vehicles than this van have been literally blown off the highway around here by winds less powerful than these."

Runnels held onto the dash with one hand and gripped the side of his seat with the other. He had to smile to himself at the irony of the situation. He had pulled off a perfect escape from prison and it looked like he would die in a storm. He couldn't be stopped now; he had to get away, to Mexico, to his world of beautiful women and fast cars. He couldn't take one more day of being locked up.

Suddenly, as if a sign from God, Runnels brightened as he saw a road sign that said El Noche -- 3 miles. His luck was holding; he would make it. A stronger blast of wind rocked the little van.

"I gotta pull over Runnels, find some type of shelter from this wind. We're going to be blown off the highway, if I don't"

"Can't do that man. You have to keep fighting it, Kramer, you can do it," encouraged the former prisoner slapping the sweating driver on the back. "We're almost there, only another three miles and we're home free. Hold on, Kramer, think of that million dollars. You get me there and all that beautiful money is yours."

"Well---," Kramer knew he had to stop, but the thought of all that money made him hesitate. "Man, if this wind hits us just right, that money ain't gonna do me no good."

Runnels looked back at Number 35 who was still sitting quietly, no recognizable expression on his broad, placid face. That man's in another world all by himself, thought Runnels.

Number 35 was staring out the windows, but he was not seeing the terrain around them. Instead he was looking at the huge walls of a mighty city, a city in flames as a massive monster of a figure stood on top of the walls and screamed maniacal laughter as he shook his huge fists toward the heavens. The field around him was littered with the dead and dying, as creatures out of his worst nightmare slowly stalked him and his men.

He could feel his lungs pump life-giving oxygen into his tired frame as he and his men braced themselves for another onslaught of the nightmarish creatures that milled about the field between them and the wall. He wasn't sure that they could withstand another wave of those creatures. The last one had cost him over half of his warriors, who even now lay silent on the dark and blood ground before him.

All might have been lost had not there suddenly been a mighty blast of trumpets which could be heard even over the sounds of war. He had turned to see a huge cloud heading directly toward the city; standing atop the cloud was the great Anu, his father, terrible in all his warlike glory. From each of the great God's hands powerful bolts of lightning arced to the ground to cut bloody swaths of death and destruction through the massed creatures. Surrounding the war chariot of Anu was the cream of Annunaki power. This was the moment, the do or die period. They would either win or lose completely.

As Romar watched in fascination, the giant Asmodeus sprang from his position on the wall and flew like a missile toward the great Anu. With a clap of thunder that could be heard for hundreds of miles, the two brothers closed for battle. Mighty blows that would have shattered mountains were rained on each other, to be shrugged off like playful slaps. Terrible energies that could have laid waste to the planet were released; massive gaping wounds appeared only to close immediately. The battle was to the death, between creatures that could not die.

Number 35 was pulled from his musings by an unusually violent gust of wind. It was clear from his eyes that he was very much aware of his surroundings. His companions failed to notice the change in the normally placid figure.

"Do the best you can," encouraged Runnels. "We can make it."

Suddenly, Kramer twisted the wheel and swore loudly as the van skidded and an unusually forceful gust of wind hit the van broadside. The steering wheel was ripped from Kramer's hands and the van was literally tossed into the air and swirled like a leaf in the wind. The three occupants were tossed around the inside of the van like straws in the wind. Kramer screamed as his seat belt snapped. The van was thrown nose first into the hillside and slammed over on the driver's side. The world went black for all its' occupants.

Mace Runnels regained consciousness to the sound of rain pounding on the side of the van with no idea of long he had been out. Mace, himself, was hanging sideways in his seat, held in place by his seat belt. Slowly, he took stock of himself and his surroundings. He had a hell of a headache, but other than that he felt in one piece. A cracked windshield was allowing a steady stream of cold water to enter the vehicle, which had already soaked his pants. The only other sound was the ticking of the engine as it cooled.

Slowly, Runnels struggled to unfasten his seat belt and allowed gravity to pull him upright. His first act was to check on the condition of his companions. Kramer was moaning softly, one leg twisted oddly under him, his face a mass of blood. Number 35 appeared to be uninjured but he had been knocked out in the crash. He dangled from the arm that was still handcuffed to the seat. Painfully, Runnels reached into his pocket and removed the handcuff keys that Kramer has slipped him before leaving the prison. He gently unlocked the cuffs, freeing Number 35 arms from the seat. Straining, he lowered the bigger man to a more comfortable position.

Making sure that Number 35 was breathing normally, Runnels

turned to Kramer who was moaning louder.

"Runnels----Runnels, where are you, man." groaned the driver, trying, with little success, to pull himself up.

Runnels crawled over to kneel by the driver.

"How you doing Kramer, my man?" he asked gently, running his hands slowly over Kramer's heaving chest.

Kramer, again, tried to pull himself into a sitting position, but finally he hugged his sides and sank back against side of the van. Runnels was sure that the driver had several fractured ribs and it didn't take a doctor to see that at least one leg was badly broken.

"I hurt, man. I hurt. My insides are on fire, breathing hurts. You gotta help me, Mace. I gotta get to El Noche and get my million bucks," he moaned, reaching up to grab Runnels by the shirtfront.

"There, there, Kramer. Don't excite yourself. It'll make it worse. Can you get up?"

Kramer coughed and Runnels saw blood on Kramer's lips. He'd probably broken a rib and it pierced his lung, thought the killer. He's gonna die, thought Runnels.

"No man, I can't move. I think my leg is broken. You gotta help me out so we can get to El Noche." he coughed again, "I gotta get my million bucks. Gonna travel, see the world."

Runnels looked out through the cracked windows, hoping to see the light of an approaching car, but saw only darkness and rain. He slammed his fist into the rear seat in frustration. Without a hospital, it was clear to Runnels that Kramer would die.

"Damn, what a time for a wreck. So close and yet so far," sighed the convict.

"Kramer, you shit, why weren't you more careful!" he swore, racking his brain for a solution.

He'd obviously have to walk the rest of the way to town and freedom. Of course, he couldn't walk three damn miles in this hellish storm with a cripple slowing him down. Unfortunately, he also knew that Kramer had a big mouth; he'd spill the beans if any pressure was put on him. With a sigh, he pulled Agent Spector's pistol from his waistband.

Thumbing back the hammer, he placed the barrel of the pistol against the side of Kramer's head.

"Sorry guy, but you're just a burden to me now. I can't afford to be slowed down. I'd take hours getting you into El Noche. I can't afford to lose that much time. At the same time, I can't afford to have anyone find you and figure out that a prisoner escaped. So--------."

Kramer's face was a picture of fear. In a panic, he weakly raised one hand and tried to push Runnels' gun away from his head. Even that much effort elicited a groan of pain from the injured driver.

"Wait, wait, man. I helped you. Without me you'd still be a prisoner. You promised that I'd get my million dollars for helping you. You can't kill me. You can't, you promised," he pleaded.

Runnels shrugged and slapped Kramer's hand away.

"Sorry Kramer, but you really didn't think we'd really pay you a million dollars once you had done your part when we could spend about .30 cents for a bullet, did you? But, for what it's worth, you really do have my thanks."

With his normal smile firmly in place, Runnels pulled the trigger, splattering Kramer's brains across the side of the vehicle. The acrid smell of cordite filled the van. Quickly, he checked the driver to make sure he was dead, though it was hardly a question with pieces of his brain splattered on the window behind him. Next, Runnels searched the body, transferring Kramer's wallet, keys and other useful items to his own pockets. With a wide grin, he found his favorite weapon attached to Kramer's belt, a long blade folding hunting knife. This, he slipped into his side pocket.

His mood considerably brightened, Runnels set about gathering any possible assets. Humming to himself, he pawed through the things scattered around the inside of the van until he found what he sought, a package containing a spare correctional officer's uniform. Silently, he gave Kramer an atta boy. The driver seemed to have thought of everything. Runnels couldn't very well wander around the area wearing his prison uniform. Ripping open the package, in seconds, Mace Runnels looked like a very professional correctional officer.

"You planned well, Kramer," he said, sketching a salute in the direction of the corpse. "Too bad you didn't plan on dying."

Looking around the van one last time, Runnels turned his attention to Number 35, who was still out.

"Sorry, big guy, I've got nothing against you. I really wish I could take you with me, but you'd just slow me down as well."

For several second Runnels weighed the pistol he still held in his hand, contemplating the unconscious prisoner sprawled in a heap in front of him. The smart thing to do was to kill Number 35 just as he had Kramer, which would insure that no one alive in the area would know that Runnels had even been in the van. With this weather it would probably be a day or two at a minimum before the wreck was discovered. In that period of time, he would be safely in Mexico.

But on the other hand, Number 35 had never done anything to hurt him. As a fellow prisoner, there was a code of conduct expected from Runnels. Though he wouldn't admit it, as cold as Runnels was toward everyone else, he actually felt some kind of bond with the big man. Finally, he shook his head, sticking the pistol into his waistband.

"Number 35, or whoever you are, I really ought to cap you too, but you're a con, like me. Hope you do O.K., big guy, but you gotta understand it's every man for himself. I hope you understand."

Runnels started to crawl to the front of the van and paused once again, looking back at Number 35.

"I don't even know your name, my man. But I really do wish you no harm. Maybe we'll meet again."

Satisfied that he had prepared as well as he could, he found that the door on his side was jammed and the window would now lower. Finally, Runnels braced his back against the seat and knocked out the passenger window with several hard kicks. Carefully, taking care to avoid the fragments of shattered glass, he worked his way out of the wrecked van, gasping in surprise as he felt the full force of the rain and wind without the van for protection. For a moment he hesitated as if uncertain of what to do, but then pulling his collar up as high as he could, the dapper killer vanished into the storm. Number 35 was left to the mercy of the elements.

Runnels was soaking wet and mud covered before he had traveled 50 feet. The road, which was seldom kept up, as it should have been was almost completely covered by mud and debris blown across it by the unprecedented winds. Every few feet he lost his footing in the slippery mud and fell. At this rate, he thought, no one will know if I am a correctional officer or a mud man. Doggedly, he kept getting back to his unsteady feet and almost clawing his way through the elements toward El Noche.

So intent was Runnels on getting to the freedom that he had come to believe that El Noche represented for him, that his normally superb danger warning, mental radar wasn't working. So it was that he didn't notice the shadowy figure standing quietly beside a tree along the side of the road. The almost hurricane force of the wind and rain seemed not to bother the mysterious figure.

The first warning the killer had of any danger was the blow that knocked him completely off his feet and sent him sliding and rolling almost twenty feet in the direction from which he had come. His senses scrambled somewhat by the force of the blow; Runnels lay for a long moment in the mud, the rain pounding on his unprotected face, the wind tearing at his clothing.

Finally, shakily, Runnels pulled himself painfully to his feet and dropped into a martial arts stance. He knew that someone, or something, had hit him, but he still had no idea who it might have been or where this person was now. Squinting against the wind, blowing sand and driving rain, his cobra like eyes searched the darkness for his foe. Always ready for a fight, he was in full killing mode. Slowly, he sidestepped, circling to find his enemy. He saw no one.

Suddenly, he was knocked rolling again. Like a cat, Runnels hit the ground, rolled and sprang back to his feet, striking out with a powerful, bone-breaking sidekick. He felt only air. Recovering, he dropped into a defensive posture. Once again, he could see no one.

"Who's there!" he screamed in frustration, drawing his pistol and once again circling to find his enemy. "Where are you?"

He was answered only by the shrieking wind and the driving rain. Again, he was hit a smashing blow that knocked him almost senseless. The force of this blow knocked him end over end through the air. He landed face down in the mud alongside the road, the pistol lost in the process.

"Where is he?" demanded a deep voice that seemed to come from all directions at once.

Runnels raised his head cautiously, spitting a mouthful of mud out in the process as he wiped the rain from his eyes. Not able to rise yet, very slowly, he glanced in every direction, but he still could see no one. The night was absolutely pitch black, not a sign of anyone could he see.

"Once more, criminal, where is he?" came the thundering voice, as Runnels was jerked to his feet and tossed down the brush covered, muddy slope.

"I don't know what you're talking about. Who are you looking for?" demanded Runnels as he slowly raised himself to his knees.

Runnels was suddenly picked up by the back of his jacket and hurled another thirty feet to land on his head in a large muddy area further down the slope from the road. Panicking, he again struggled to regain his feet as his gasping mouth took in a large scoop of mud.

Without warning, Runnels was pulled roughly to his feet and hurled through the air again, to land in a muddy heap some yards away. Slowly, he raised his head to see before him two thick, powerful legs. Surprised, he raised one hand to wipe the mud from his eyes to see that it was an Indian that stood before him. Gathering his diminishing strength, Runnels rolled to one side, and then sprang to his feet.

"O.K. Geronimo, if it's a fight you want, it's a fight I'll give you," snarled the killer as he circled around his opponent.

With a mighty yell, and a flurry of mud, Runnels sprang high into the air and lashed out with his left foot at the Indian's vulnerable throat; a swift, deadly maneuver that would quickly end the fight. To his complete surprise, the Indian languidly slapped his foot away as if swatting an insect. Runnels cart wheeled through the air to, once again, crash head first into the mud. The sound of splashing told him that the Indian had come to stand before him again.

"One last time, white-eye, where is he!" demanded the Indian, reaching out one big hand to pull Runnels back to his feet by the back of his jacket.

Runnels responded by trying to slam his right elbow into the Indian's stomach. The force of the blow shook Runnels to his toes as it felt like he had rammed his elbow into a brick wall. Seeming to feel no effect from what should have been a crippling blow, the Indian simply tossed Runnels some twenty feet through the air. This time, the flying killer slammed into a small tree, uprooting it by the force with which he hit it.

With a major effort, Runnels pulled his battered body back to his feet. He stood for a few seconds, swaying groggily; he could feel his eyes swelling and taste the blood that flowed down his face. He slowly rubbed his sleeve across his puffy lips.

"Who is it you want, Indian?" he managed to ask, before he slipped to one knee, his strength fading rapidly.

"The one you arrived with. Him I have been waiting for longer than you have lived," thundered the menacing figure, striding toward the groggy killer.

Runnels shook his head slowly, struggling back to his feet.

"I got no idea who you're talking about Indian, but I do know that nobody lays his hands on me and lives. I'm Mace Runnels."

With blinding speed, using the last dregs of his energy, Runnels lashed out with a stiffened hand toward the Indian's solar plexus. Runnels had killed bigger men than this upstart Indian with this blow. He intended to rip the Indian's heart out through his chest. This time, Runnels' blow connected, the Indian made a strange sound and fell backward. Having expended so much energy, Runnels felt nothing but jubilation as he fell to his knees. For several minutes, he simply rested and panted, waiting for the pain in his ribs to ease enough for him to get back to his feet.

Having regained some of his strength, Runnels struggled back to his feet and turned toward where he had dropped the Indian. He fully intended to make sure that the red skinned son of a bitch was dead. Slogging through the mud, he stumbled over to where he knew the Indian had fallen, but he found nothing. Frantically, he splashed around searching for the body. He found nothing.

"Nooooooo!" he screamed, it was impossible. No one had ever survived that blow.

Suddenly, his danger radar kicked in and he spun around, almost losing his balance. The Indian stood tall and strong before him, massive arms folded across his chest.

"Looking for something pale face?" asked the Indian, a calm smile across his broad face.

Screaming like a banshee, Runnels launched himself at the Indian, his fingers outstretched like claws. His world had narrowed until there was just one thought on his mind---kill. He would literally over power his opponent.

Runnels was so far over the edge, that it really didn't register on his crazed mind that the Indian simply slapped him aside with a quick movement of one powerful arm. Getting back to his feet, the assassin felt around for a weapon, finding a strong stick about three feet long. Holding it like a lance, the crazed man came running at his opponent, intending to run him through.

His face still covered by the gentle smile, the Indian reached out one hand and simply grabbed the stick. Runnels stopped in his tracks as if he had hit a brick wall. With a surge of unbelievable power, the Indian used the stick to toss Runnels some fifteen feet away. Runnels slammed into the ground on his back, stars dancing before his swollen eyes.

Weakly, the assassin tried to roll over on his stomach to regain his feet, but lacked even the strength to do that simple movement. He had a single moment of lucidity when he realized that he would die on this muddy hillside. Ironic, he thought, he had killed the world's best and most powerful, in the best cities in the world, for millions. Now in a two-bit town, in a sand hill of a state, he was dying at the hands of an ignorant

Indian. He was recalled from his mental wondering by the sight of the Indian leaning over him.

"Where is he?" asked the Indian, gently.

"Who!" demanded Runnels fighting against the pain in his damaged ribs, "Who are you looking for?"

"I look for he who traveled with you," stated the Indian, "He who I have waited for these many years. Where is he?"

Runnels shook his head weakly, his will to fight gone.

"I don't know. I don't know. Honestly, I really don't know who you're talking about. I came in a prison van with a Federal Agent, a Correctional Officer and a crazy man. I don't know who else you could be talking about," he mumbled.

"Where is the vehicle you came in?" demanded the thunderous voice, as Runnels felt a hand grab him by the front of his tattered shirt and lift him easily from the sucking mud that cradled his bruised body.

The beaten assassin weakly flailed his left arm, pointing back toward the road. At the same time, he slipped Kramer's knife from his pocket and flipped open the folding blade with his right hand.

"Please, no more. It's back there on the road. Short ways back that way, toward the hill."

As the Indian prepared to drop him back to the muddy ground, Runnels slashed at his stomach with the knife. In a movement too rapid for the eye to follow, the Indian let go of his shirt and grabbed the knife hand. Slowly, the Indian's large powerful hand tightened on Runnels' smaller hand. The pain was terrible. Moaning in spite of himself, in total desperation, Runnels struck at the Indian's face with the side of his left hand. For a third time, the Indian slapped away his most deadly martial arts moves as if he had been an amateur.

Deciding to end the encounter, with a quick movement of his fingers, the Indian crushed Runnels' hand. The bones popped like firecrackers. The assassin's terrible scream echoed through the night. The deadly knife fell from the useless fingers to splash in the mud at their feet. The Indian released his grip to allow Runnels to fall back into the ever-present mud. Instinctively, the assassin struggled back to his knees.

"You've ruined my hand, you bastard," he moaned, trying to rise to his feet, but falling back to his knees. Slowly, he bent forward to rest his forehead in the mud, cradling his destroyed right hand against his heaving chest.

With no expression on his broad face, the Indian reached down and grabbed a handful of Runnels' plastered hair. With no sign of effort, he lifted the assassin back to his knees by his hair. Reaching around the wounded man's head with his other hand, the Indian grabbed Runnels' chin and gave a quick jerk with both hands. The pop of Runnel's neck breaking was like the snapping of a rotten stick, one of the deadliest killers in the history of the underworld went completely limp. The Indian released his grip to let the dead man fall face forward back into the mud.

"Evil ones, such as yourself, should be destroyed whenever possible. You kill when you could preserve life. As you do, so shall be done to you. It is the law," said the Indian as he step back and drew the night around himself like a cloak to slowly fade from view.

Runnels was left lying face down in the ever rising mud. Unmourned, his grave would forever be unmarked. No one marked his passing, as he was alone except for the keening of the wind and the pounding rain. There was no sign that there had ever been any other person there, no sign of the battle that had raged for so long.

Runnels had died as he had lived, alone. By the end of the driving rainstorm, the mud would have deepened to the point that his body would be completely covered, sort of a natural burial. No one would ever see Mace Runnels again, nor know of his passing. He had spent his life becoming the perfect killing machine and had been at the top of his chosen profession until, on a dark stormy night, he had tried to pit his killing talents against those of a demigod. In a contest between a man and a god, the god will always win.

CHAPTER SEVENTEEN

"He oughta be here soon, don't cha think, boss," said Martony as he leaned forward to rest his arms on the table, a glass of whiskey sitting near his hand. "I mean, he should have been here a couple of hours ago. He's gotta be here soon, unless something has gone wrong."

The only sound in the room was from the pounding of the rain against the windows. The other people in the rooms sat quietly, nursing their own private thoughts. The lamps were turned down low and the fire was reduced to glowing coals. Molena was nursing a drink of aged Scotch from a bottle Petey had found under the bar.

"With this weather, you really can't tell." shrugged the Drug Czar. "True, according to the time schedule, he should have been here two hours ago. But there are a hundred things that could have happened to delay him."

"So what do we do?" asked Martony, rubbing his thick neck slowly, "This place really gives me the creeps."

Molena sipped at his glass, his hard eyes flickering around the room, pausing for a moment to glance at his aide.

"Afraid of that old lady's monsters, Fingers?" chuckled his boss.

"We wait; it's all we can do. There's no way to contact him, so we just sit here like big fat pigeons until he gets here."

He paused for a long moment, his eyes flickering in the firelight.

"Nick, there's no question of doing anything else. He knows too much about our operations," he said in a low tone of voice. "We have to make sure that we either get Runnels out of the country or silence him for good. We simply cannot take the chance of the law getting him again."

Nick Martony leaned back in his chair as he considered what his boss was telling him. It was being proposed that he, Nick Martony take out the top assassin in the criminal world, possibly in history. Mace Runnels had survived over forty attempts on his life and always walked away the victor. He had also always tracked down his would be killers and disposed of them in very imaginative, painful ways. If he succeeded in removing Runnels as a threat to the organization, he would be a legend in the families; he might even be elevated to the Council. But if he failed, he would die horribly.

He glanced up to find Molena's eyes drilling into him.

"Well, really I'm not sure I can take him, boss. The kid's the best I've ever seen. I might get one chance, and if I blow that one, he'll kill all of us."

Molena reached across the table and grabbed Martony's arm.

"Understand me, Fingers. You have to do it. If we can get Runnels out of the country; then well and good. We can dispose of him in Mexico at our leisure. If we can't get him out, then there is no option; he has to die before the authorities can catch him again.

This "rescue" if you want to call it that, was actually authorized by the Council. The plan was to spring him from the prison and then kill him. The big boys feel that he knows too much about too many people. If we don't kill him, the Council will send people after, not only Runnels, but us as well. It truly is a life or death situation."

With a deep sigh, Martony, reached beneath his coat and made sure that his gun was lose in his holster. He had been telling Molena the truth; he would only get one chance.

"How about that Sheriff?" whispered Martony, glancing around the room at this enforced companions. "I doubt he is going to stand by while I gun Runnels down and shooting him like a dog is the only chance I've got to get him."

Molena shrugged and reached for the untouched glass of whiskey on the table.

"Tiny Joe can take care of the county cop if he does become a problem. But he'll probably still be out running around the county when Runnels arrives. Actually, if we can't get Runnels into Mexico, for some reason, I thought we'd have him come in here, maybe for some coffee before hitting the road and kill him in here."

Martony glanced toward the counter where big Petey was making another pot of coffee.

"Boss, there's about a dozen people in here. We can't kill them all, can we?"

Molena smiled a small smile.

"Remember the old days, Fingers? If we have to do it, we just kill Runnels here and then torch the joint. What with these oil lamps and the big fire, folks will just think that an unfortunate accident happened. Besides, most of these folk're old, who'll miss them?"

Molena planned his plan, but on this night, more than one set of plans had and would go awry. On this night, the gods were restless. On this night, the evil ones spoken of in myth and story would be roaming the earth. On this night, a door that should never be opened would slowly begin to move. On this night, there would be a test to determine the depth of one man's courage and heart. Passing the test was not a certain thing.

PART III

THE OLD MISSION

CHAPTER EIGHTEEN

El Noche Valley was a very unusual place in more ways than one. Dominating the valley was massive Devil's Hill, a massive mound of earth and stone that rose from the lower ridges that almost encircled the little valley. On the east side of Devil's Hill was a large area of flat ground encompassing perhaps five acres of good rich soil. Due to an unusual fluke of nature, this particular five-acre area was well watered by an underground stream that came to the surface in the center of the old Mission.

Everyone in the area that knew about the small grouping of ancient buildings that perched on the east side of Devil's Hill called them the Old Spanish Mission. There were very few ruins in the general area of the valley; those that were found were always in a very deteriorated condition. However, the Old Spanish Mission, though this was not exactly an accurate description, looked like the early inhabitants had walked away only yesterday. The old buildings were so old that no one really knew who has built them, but it was almost like the wind and rain were completely ignored.

Though it was the a common belief that the Spanish had built the Mission, actually, when the earliest of the Spanish Explorers had arrived in the area in their search for gold, they had found the Old Mission already a long deserted ruin. A thorough search of the buildings and the surrounding country had uncovered no information on the inhabitants of the Mission. Added to the mystery presented by the large ornate buildings in the middle of an otherwise deserted country, the Spanish were also puzzled by the fact that no Indians lived in the valley, even though water and grass were plentiful. By all rights, a large population should have inhabited the valley. A record of the location of the puzzling buildings had been dispatched back to the Governor of Spanish America, but a roving band of Indians made sure that the report never reached its' intended destination.

For centuries the buildings had remained deserted, like an animal crouching on the plateau, sealed up tight against both nesting animals and two legged invaders. Though to be truthful, no one had ever seen an animal anywhere on the plateau. In the late 1880s people from El Noche, led by the local Catholic Priest, gained access to the main chapel building and renovated it for use as a church for the surrounding ranchers. With the years of dirt and grime removed, the building was absolutely beautiful and as ornate as any European Chapel. For many years' time, it was a well-respected place of worship and spiritual comfort, staffed by two priests and a dozen lay brothers.

It was in the 1930s that the first recorded trouble came to the El Noche Mission. Oh, the horror probably had always been there in the valley, watching and waiting for a chance to strike, but for some reason, the horror had long lain dormant. No one ever knew what began the killing cycle, but it always seemed to begin the week before Halloween.

The first death was that of one of the serving lay brothers. Brother Timothy, he was called within the Order. He was a tall, muscular man, popular with the parishioners, fond of exercising by working for hours on end in the large garden plot maintained just outside the Mission wall. He also was a man of great curiosity, so when he unearthed the first carving, he avidly began to dig for more. It was almost dark when he found the big one. Almost two feet tall, the statute represented a creature that Brother Timothy had never seen. From the moment that he unearthed the figure, he felt it was Satanic. He felt that it was more than a statute; he felt that it was alive. He placed it on the altar that night when he went to late prayers.

The unusual carving; that may have been what began the cycle all over again. But, not one ever realized that there might have been a connection. That night, Brother Timothy had placed the statuette on the altar for God to take charge of as he said his evening prayers. At the late hour, he was the only one praying in the Chapel, which was not unusual for Brother Timothy, for he loved the solitude of the ornate Chapel. He was asking his God to protect him from the evil he had begun to sense when he heard the footsteps of someone coming up behind him.

Turning, he had seen that one of the other lay brothers had entered the chapel. However, he had also noticed that the Brother was wearing a solid black robe, instead of the normal brown one. The new comer also had his cowl pulled low over his face, so it was impossible to see what he looked like. Timothy was puzzled, as he had not heard of any visitors to the Mission, but it was the custom of the Order that all were welcome to worship in the main Chapel.

Brother Timothy had risen from his prayers and turned to face the visitor.

"Welcome, Brother. I know not who you are, but you are welcome in God's House, as are all. I am Brother Timothy. Come and join with me in prayer."

The Black Robe had walked past the Holy Water Fount without notice and also failed to kneel toward the altar as was customary. Slowly he came down the long aisle to stop in front of the puzzled Brother Timothy.

"Brother, you do not kneel before our Lord in his own house?" had questioned Brother Timothy, brow furrowed.

The Black Robed figure had leaned forward and tossed back his cowl to reveal his face. When the stranger had straightened, Brother Timothy had found himself staring into the face of a creature from hell. With his own bulging eyes, he was looking into face of the model for the statuette he had placed on the altar. He was looking into the face of death.

"This is not your puny Lord's house, human. This is the ancestral home of the infernal one--- the ancient god of evil. It is you Christians that have desecrated what you do not understand. "

With that the creature grabbed Brother Timothy in his claw like hands and threw him across the room, to crash heavily against the far wall. Ignoring the moaning human, he then walked slowly forward and reverently lifted the statuette from the altar where Brother Timothy had placed it. Turning, he made for the front doors of the Chapel.

Seeing the desecration of the sanctity of the altar, Brother Timothy rose to his feet and charged after the demon. With a mighty he effort leaped from the top outer step and slammed into the back of the monstrous creature and propelled him across the courtyard as if shot from a cannon. The statuette went spinning across the pavement.

Rushing over to the fallen idol, Brother Timothy grabbed it up into his arms and rushed back toward the Chapel. He skidded to a stop when he saw that a second demon crouched in the doorway. He turned to run when the first demon came charging back at him. The creature caught him before he could go two steps.

"You die now, human." The creature had roared as he had lifted the struggling Brother into the air.

With a superhuman effort, he had literally ripped Brother Timothy in half, the statuette falling to the ground. Hurling the dead human aside, the creature had scooped the statuette into his arms and started back toward the exit. Suddenly he had stopped and turned toward the other demon.

"Kill those who would desecrate the home of the Master," he had ordered.

He had then turned and faded into the night with his prize.

For the next hour, the second demon had roamed the Mission, killing all those he found. The bodies were left where they had fallen, as a symbol to those who had dared to mouth those hateful things or worshipped other gods in the House of Asmodeus. It was truly the home of death, not of life. By dawn, nothing lived on the plateau.

The next attempt by the outside world to interfere with Devil's Hill was the establishment in 1943 of a top secret monitoring station on the summit of Devil's Hill. The purpose of the station had been to monitor the Manhattan Project tests to be conducted at White Sands. The tests had gone well, however, the Station reported some unusual radiation readings immediately after the test. Shortly thereafter, all contact with the Station had been lost. When security teams had arrived, the Station was completely deserted. The entire staff had vanished without a trace.

The Station had continued to be used as a government facility until the end of 1993. In the era of budget cuts, the land had been turned back to the county. The county tried to use it as a storage facility for the highway department, but things kept disappearing. After two security guards had vanished in one single night, the county had abandoned the base. In 1994, a private corporation had rented the base for research purposes. On Halloween Night in 1995, the full staff had again vanished without a trace. The property was donated back to the Church.

CHAPTER NINETEEN

In the main Chapel of the Old Spanish Mission, a group of individuals sat in the front pews, listening avidly to an older man who stood before the altar. The leader was a tall, slightly stooped individual of advanced years. His longish white hair was in considerable disarray due to his habit of running his right hand through his hair when thinking.

Though to the outside world these fifteen people represented a mysterious religious cult that always went robed, several of the individuals in the room were top scientists in several disciplines. The idea for the robes had been developed from the garb of the sole caretaker who lived in the Mission keeping it in repair for the Mother Church.

The idea had been to keep the curious outside world from meddling in what the scientists believed was very important work. Where the presence of several imminent scientists could be expected to draw attention, one more religious cult would not excite anyone's interest. Currently, except for the always-silent caretaker, they were all wearing jeans and heavy work shoes. One or two were covered with dirt as if they had been tunneling in the earth.

"There's no question that something is buried beneath this Mission. Our sonar tests have revealed the existence of a deep tunnel running from the front courtyard at a forty-five degree angle. Additionally, something has certainly disturbed the ether. It began this morning and has been getting stronger," stated an older man sitting in the front pew.

"Thank you, Dr. Carter," stated the middle-aged man standing in front of the altar; "I think that is probably one of the most unnerving signs that some danger is approaching."

He stood, with arms folded, on hand rubbing his chin. Suddenly he turned to his right, looking at a rather plain middle-aged woman sitting quietly by herself.

"Madame Sasha, have your methods revealed anything new?"

The woman looked up at the mention of her name.

"I have consulted my spirit guides and even they are afraid of what can be sensed here. There is an evil force that seems to emanate from this location. But it isn't a force, as we understand force, but rather a field of some type. I ---I can't find the exact location of the main source, but it is close."

"Keep trying, my dear." encouraged Dr. Bonner.

Immediately, he turned to the other female among the group.

"Sheila, any word on your sister, yet?" he asked softly.

Her crimson locks framing her face like a halo, lovely Sheila Bennett nodded slowly, a perturbed look on her lovely face.

"Amanda should have been here hours ago. I checked in town and found that there had been no sign of her. But the weather is bad and getting worse by the minute. You know that we have always had a special mental bond. I tried to establish our special mental contact simply to determine where she is and found nothing. It is as if she no longer exists. Gentlemen, you don't know my sister. There is nothing on this earth that she could not handle.

Something's happened to Amanda. I don't know what and I don't know how or where. But I am sure of the fact that she is somewhere close by, but in serious trouble. I get the feeling that she is somehow restrained."

The leader turned to the left and singled out another of his followers.

"Dr. Sonnerman, is it possible to calibrate our equipment to home in more closely on the source of Sasha's energy field?"

Dr. Parker Sonnerman, a tall lanky individual with a full beard stood and glanced around the room.

"We can certainly try. However, without knowing more about the nature of the energy field, it is difficult to properly calibrate our equipment."

"Please try." encourage Bonner as he turned back to Madame Sasha.

"Sasha, could you possibly see what your spirit guides can tell you of Amanda Bennett? He asked.

"Dr. Bonner, correct me if I am wrong," she said addressing the leader, "but as I understand it, Amanda Bennett has no idea that Sheila, or herself for that matter, have usable extra sensory perception or that Sheila monitors her sister on a periodic basis. Correct?"

Dr. Harold Bonner nodded without comment.

"If," continued Sasha, "Amanda Bennett was fully aware of her channel of communication with Sheila, then much like the gain on a radio, then I could possibly use that communications channel to find Amanda. However, since she has no idea of her potential, then it would be like beaming a signal to a turned off television. Very little would happen. In fact in my attempts to find her, I might make matters worse, she might think that she was losing her mind."

"Just a minute, Dr. Bonner." interrupted a stout individual sitting in a rear pew.

Dr. Bonner raised one eyebrow and nodded for the gentleman to speak.

"Dr. Bonner, gentlemen and ladies," he began, "I suggest that we end this so-called project and go back to some real science."

"What exactly do you mean, Dr. Peterson?" asked Dr. Bonner.

"Dr. Bonner, you asked me to take part in a serious investigation into the after effects caused by the Manhattan Project tests. You showed me what I took to be real proof that the effects of the Manhattan Project Tests caused some type of rift in the space-time continuum. I joined based on this hypothesis."

Dr. Emile Peterson, one of the world's foremost authorities in radiation got to his feet and walked toward the front of the chapel.

"Dr. Bonner, I agreed to help you. I expected us to spend months taking readings and doing experiments in the area where the tests actually took place. Instead, I found that we were operating from this ancient rock heap. The early nuclear tests were on the other side of a mountain range, for God's sake. What can we hope to find here. I have asked this question since the day that I arrived at this rock.

Even so, I agreed to continue with the project. That was eight months ago. Instead of very serious scientific studies, I have watched what was supposed to be a serious examination of atomic after effects degenerate into some type of circus for fortune tellers, no offense meant Madame Sasha, so called attempts to track some energy source with spirit guides and God knows what all.

Now, Dr. Lars Sonnerman, a world-class nuclear physicist is going to seriously try to find a source we only know of as a result of Madame Sash's alleged ESP. We have now just heard a discussion of trying to make some type of mental contact with someone who is not here.

It's crazy, it's worse than crazy, it's insane and I will no longer be a part of whatever you think you are doing."

Dr. Bonner shook his head slowly, nodded thoughtfully and opened his mouth to speak, but his attention was drawn to a dark corner of the Chapel by a gasp from Sheila.

"Look, over there. Something is happening. I see flickering lights."

All eyes turned to the corner indicated and all saw a mass of sparkling tiny lights. At first the blinking of the tiny lights was random, but soon the lights began to form a recognizable pattern. As if there was an unseen struggle taking place, the figure seemed to fade in and out of existence. Finally, after several long minutes of struggle, the recognizable figure of an Indian stood before them.

Slowly, the Indian raised one arm and pointed across the room at Sheila.

"You of the flame hair, you are the one." he said in a deep hollow sounding spectral voice. "It is you that must go and bring the Other to this place of evil. You are his only hope and he is your only hope for survival. You must act quickly for the ancient evil one has awakened and even now has called his minions to come to him."

Slowly, he began to fade from sight.

"Wait!" yelled Sheila, running from her place to stand before the ethereal Indian. "Who is the Other? Where is he? Who's the evil one?"

As she watched, the Indian faded quickly from view. Only his voice remained.

"Seek the Other in the storm: on the road. Hurry, for you must get to him before the evil one does."

Sheila stood staring at the spot where the Indian had materialized; she had no idea what to say. The spell of amazement was broken by the sound of slow applause. Sheila spun around on her heel and saw it was Dr. Peterson that was sneering at Dr. Bonner and applauding.

"Bravo, Dr. Bonner, bravo. I should have expected something like this from you. After all one of your specialties is holographic research. Did you have the holographic Indian rigged up in case one of your disciples got out of line? Well, it didn't impress me. I'm wise to your tricks."

The stout scientist held up one finger and pointed it at Dr. Bonner.

"I am telling you right now Bonner that if you don't give me some rational explanation for all this mumbo jumbo, I am leaving and filing a report regarding this abortion of a project and your lack of scientific methods with the National Scientific Board. I happen to know that this project was funded by one of the NSB's grants. After I get through talking to them about how you are spending their money, you won't be able to get approval for an experiment into anything."

Dr. Bonner held up one hand to stem the flow of Dr. Peterson's speech. With a deep sigh, he walked forward and sat on the top most of the two steps that led up to the altar.

"Dr. Peterson, you were recruited late. It's my fault that, due to the lack of time, I didn't fully brief you on certain things. You also don't know the history of this place or my involvement with it. In fact, I have told none of you the entire story.

First, let me say that I have no idea who, or what, that Indian was or how he came to appear here. Next, I am afraid that I took advantage of all of your scientific curiosity regarding radioactivity tests. Except for you, Miss Bennett. You know more than the others about what this is about."

"Well, tell us then. Give us some rational reason for some of the most prominent scientists in the world acting like children afraid of the dark." snapped the angry scientist, dropping into a nearby empty pew.

"Not afraid of the dark, itself, Dr. Peterson, but rather what happens when darkness falls." observed Dr. Bonner from his seat.

Dr. Bonner rubbed his chin slowly and tried to decide how to begin his story. If not handled properly this minor mutiny could mean the end of his research and perhaps the end of civilization. He opened his mouth to speak, but was interrupted by one of the younger members of the group.

"There is a story that has made the rounds regarding the old Monitoring Station that people disappeared there back in the 40's. Kind of the like Flight 19 that vanished in the Bermuda Triangle." offered one of the others, "Is that what this is about?"

Dr. Bonner shook his head slowly.

"No, my friends, no one actually vanished there, at least no one that I know of. The true story was so bizarre and unbelievable that it was the government that started the story regarding the staff simply disappearing to cover up what really happened."

The scientist paused while he absently rubbed his lower lip; toying with an unlit cigarette. Finally, he turned his attention back to the others in the room.

"In 1943, my father was an army officer." began Dr. Bonner, "Due to his scientific background and his friendship with Dr. Einstein; he was assigned to the Manhattan Project. He helped design the device that became the most powerful weapon the world had ever seen. I was a young physicist, just out of school and due to Dr. Einstein's personal recommendation; I had also been assigned to the project.

The first atomic tests succeeded far beyond expectations. The day of the largest and final test, my father was assigned to command the survey team stationed at Monitoring Station 14. That's the one that was located on the summit of this little mountain we are sitting on."

Dr. Bonner paused and with shaking hands pulled a cigarette from his pocket and placed it in his mouth. He absently searched for a match, but stopped when one of the others came forward and handed him a lighter. He lit the cigarette and smiled at his listeners.

"In fact the station was located in this building, though not here in the chapel."

He stopped for a moment and rubbed his lower lip with his right thumbnail.

"You see," he began, between puffs on his cigarette," Though the theory of the bomb had been fairly well determined to be workable, there was a great deal of concern about the extent of the effect of the bomb. The big question was what would happen immediately after the detonation of the bomb, would the massive release of energy result in a continuing chain reaction that would literally destroy the earth.

My father's job was to determine how far radiation would extent from ground zero. Installed in Station 14 was some of the most cutting edge sensitive equipment that the best brains in this country could design. He used to laugh that if a fly sneezed at ground zero it would blow out the speakers on top of Devil's Hill."

The old man paused in his talk for a few minutes, his deep-set eyes looking across the years to when he was a young man, so proud to be working with his father on such an important project. Back to a day when he still had real hopes of helping the world enter a better era. Sensing his pensive mood, Sheila came to sit beside him, talking one of his large, gnarled hands between hers. He favored her with a slight smile.

"Due to the need to replace an ill technician at the central facility, instead of being at Monitoring Station 14 as I had planned, I was assigned to be in the main control room the day of the test. My father was in direct radio contact with the crew stationed at ground zero right up to the minute the test took place. As expected, the after effects of the atomic blast knocked out all radio communications in the general area, but there was a second back up direct telephone line."

"Electromagnetic pulse", interrupted one of the electronic experts sitting nearby.

"Exactly," said Dr. Bonner. "At first the information regarding the strength of the radiation fan and the various types of radiation being reported back from Station 14 was in line with the earlier projections of the team. I remember that we were all so amazed that the reality was actually so close to the projections arrived at by the physicists assigned to the Manhattan Project.

The initial burst of radiation was massive at ground zero, but well within acceptable limits at Monitoring Station 14. The actual monitoring equipment was installed in a series of deeply buried rooms, carved out of the solid rock of this hill. It was theorized that due to the shielding of the rock and the earth itself, the team assigned to man the Station would be completely safe from any direct effects of the bomb, itself.

It was clear to all of us that the final test had been a complete success. The continual information being sent back from Station 14 was completely in line with our expectations regarding the levels of radiation; everything was taking place as it had been projected. However, one hour after the initial blast, my father reported a sudden surge in recorded radiation. He described it as being like a door opening and closing. During the period that he would describe as the door being opened, the radiation meters went crazy, when the door closed, the radiation dropped significantly back to previous levels."

"Bomb after effects?" asked Dr. Peterson, interested in spite of himself.

Dr. Bonner shook his head.

"No, later we considered that, but the radiation was not the same type that was released by the bomb. Wrong end of the radiation spectrum. This type of radiation was totally unlike anything that had been released by any of the previous tests, nor was this type of radiation or anything even remotely close to it later found in the ruins of Hiroshima or Nagasaki."

Again the scientist fell silent, his eyes again staring across the years.

"So what happened?" gently questioned Sheila, pulling the old man from his reverie.

"Oh, where was I, yes, my father." he began, "About two hours later, my father reported that the unusual radiation readings were back and getting stronger. Dr. Conrad, the chief of the control room team, contacted all of the other monitoring stations in the area, of which there were twenty-four, but they all reported readings within expected limits. None reported the bizarre readings similar to those from Station 14. On a hunch, Dr. Conrad had the other stations orient their monitoring equipment toward Station 14. Their equipment went totally crazy; the dials all went off the scale.

A later plotting of the data from the other stations, showed a pulsating central mass of radiation located on the south end of the test area and an area of radiation that seemed to run straight as an arrow from the central mass toward Devil's Hill. What was the most bizarre was that the central mass of radiation seemed to being square shaped, exactly like the opening and closing "door" mentioned by my father. The arrow of radiation that ran toward Station 14 was approximately twenty feet across, with clearly definable edges, like a tunnel. No one could explain it.

We were all puzzled, but merely assumed that it was just a side effect of the blast until shortly after dusk. My father and his team had been busy all afternoon gathering data and reporting it back; remember that we were in constant contact with Station 14 the entire time. It had become very clear that only Station 14 was reporting the strange readings, which were continually getting closer to Devil's Hill.

Dusk was at 6:34 that day. I'll never forget it, I had to sit and listen to what happened without being able to help."

Again, lost in his memories, Dr. Bonner lapsed into silence, simply staring off into space. Respectfully, the other all waited for him to continue. Finally, Sheila again prompted him.

"Dr. Bonner?" she said gently, "Dr. Bonner, what happened to your father?"

With a start, the scientist rejoined them mentally, "Oh, I'm sorry, lost in memories don't you know." He paused and stretched.

"Well, it was about seven that night when my father reported that strange noises were being heard in other parts of the station. There were eight scientists and eleven military at the station. All were sealed within the lead lined instrument room some forty feet below the ground.

Naturally, the rest of the station would be monitored by security devices that could be controlled from the instrument room. A security precaution, don't you know.

"Well, my father reported that over the internal speakers, he could hear sounds that seemed to be similar to voices as well as footsteps and the sounds of pounding. He naturally assumed that other personnel had been sent to relieve him and his security team. He gave instruction to break the seal on the room door and sent two armed men out to greet the new comers. The only problem was we hadn't sent any relief team.

"The shots and screams of the two men he sent out could be heard over the open line even though the closed lead lined door. I heard my father give the order to open the door in order to rescue his men."

Bonner clutched his big hands into fists and raised them above his head, his eyes squeezed tightly closed.

"You have no idea how hard I tried to warn him not to open that door. I screamed into that transmitter until my voice cracked. But for some reason, even though the connection allowed for a two-way communication line, my father seemed not to hear me.

"As clear as day, I heard the discussions in that room. He ordered his security detail to get ready and then I heard the main door slam back against the wall. After that it got very confused, I heard gunfire, explosions, screams and crashes. My father yelled orders up to the last. Then, it was all over; there was only silence, except for a strange crunching.

"The only recognizable words we had heard during the entire melee were from my father. He had screamed, "What are they?"

"Well, Dr. Conrad got on the phone and called Test Security. Within minutes, he had an entire Company of heavily armed Infantry swarming up the sides of this Hill. The Station was still secured. In fact they had to force open the outer doors of the Station, as they were still locked. Nothing moved on the first floor of the building.

"Moving carefully, the soldiers first cleared the first floor, before moving to the elevator. There were three levels below the ground level; the first elevator only went to the second level. A second smaller elevator went down to the instrument room. It was, of course, considered a top-secret area.

"On the second level below the ground, the troops found that one of the outer walls had been smashed in from the outside. Beyond the smashed wall could be seen a long narrow tunnels bored out of the solid rock. They could not see the other end of the tunnel, so they had no idea where it led. They wanted to explore the tunnel immediately, but their primary goal was the rescue of the team.

"Carefully, they descended to the last level. Death and destruction were all around. The bodies of the soldiers, which were horribly mutilated, showed that they had fought a last ditch battle before they were overpowered. My father's body was found crumpled in a corner, his chest ripped open."

He paused for a moment, his eyes tightly closed.

"Three members of the scientific staff were missing. Their bodies were never found, in spite of a massive search. The only sign of what had attacked them was a green viscous liquid, which had the same consistency as human blood. Oh, yes and there was one print found in a patch of dried blood. The print seemed to be from a biped; however, it showed that the creature which has four claws instead of toes."

"So what happened? Did the soldiers find the creature?" asked Dr. Mason, a botanist on the team.

Dr. Bonner shrugged.

"With the wartime government secrecy and the "need to know" syndrome, who knows what the government did or didn't find? I heard that the next day a heavily armed team entered the tunnel with orders to trace it to the end. No one ever spoke of what was found. However, I did find out years later that only half the members of the team ever returned. Most of those that escaped back to the surface were insane when they returned."

"Any idea of what the soldiers actually found in the tunnel, Dr. Bonner?" asked Sheila.

He looked at her with a very sad face. His answer was only one word.

"Evil."

CHAPTER TWENTY

Simon Dakkar stood straight and tall before the statue of his Master. A very much alive, though extremely angry, Amanda Bennett stood before him near a large wooden dais set into the ground. The ever-present Julia had pulled Amanda from the altar when the black cloth was raised and draped over the substituted sacrifice. While everyone watched Dakkar sacrifice the victim, Amanda had been held prisoner in a side room, her arms still bound, tied to an iron ring set into the rock above her head. The ever-present gag back in place, she had stood quietly, helplessly out of sight until the ceremony was over.

At a sign from Dakkar, Julia rejoined Amanda to free her arms from above her head. Her wrists were quickly retired behind her back. Then Amanda had been brought to stand before the scarlet robed Dakkar. The other scarlet robed figures had long since filed out of the cavern to wait for their leader outside.

"Well, my dear, I am sure that you are wondering what is happening, aren't you? As you can see, you really didn't die on the altar," he said motioning toward the dead body still sprawled on the altar behind him. "She was a local woman, who, as you can see, bore somewhat of a resemblance to you. My followers were suitably happy, of course. But, I couldn't allow you to be used for such a mundane purpose."

Amanda's eyes widened in shock at the sight of the dead girl lying on the altar: it was almost like looking in a mirror. A closer look showed that the resemblance was a result of a very artful application of theatrical make-up

"However," continued Dakkar, "I said that you would be the center piece of tonight's ceremony and you will. You see, I, though the Master of these cattle that blindly follow me, am not the real Master. No, I answer to one who is all-powerful and all knowing. He desires to meet you, my dear. You should be honored.

"He is a god, he desires you for his bride. He is a vengeful god and visits death and destruction on even the children of those who have angered him. One of your ancestors had the great misfortune to anger Asmodeus centuries ago. He desires to take his revenge on you and your sister.

"You, we sacrifice now, your sister will join you within a short time. You should be honored, as you will both serve him for all eternity"

He nodded to Julia, who went over to the dais and pressed a switch. The dais slowly moved back to reveal a circular opening in the floor. A peculiar smell wafted up from its depths. Walking closer to Amanda, Dakkar placed his hand on her shoulder, she tried to wrench away in disgust. His fingers tightened painfully into her soft flesh. Slowly, he urged her closer to the hole.

"You should be honored, my dear. The Master, himself, wants to make your acquaintance. So enjoy." he said as he gave her a hard shove. As the helpless, gagged woman toppled head first into the hole, she couldn't even scream her terror.

The dozens of scarlet robed figures stood silently awaiting their directions of Dakkar. When he walked out of the corridor to join him they began to chant, "Asmodeus, Asmodeus."

For a long time, Dakkar allowed them to vent their excitement until he judged that they were at a fever pitch. Finally, he climbed atop a chair and raised his arms for silence.

"You heard the Master's instructions! Tonight he begins his return to the world of the living. His eons of wrongful imprisonment are now at and end. Though immortal, his many thousands of years of imprisonment have sapped even his mighty powers. Now he needs our help as never before. To regain his true power, to finally break free of his eternal prison, our Lord has need of much human blood. We now need many captives to help pave the way for our Lord's freedom; we need these people to be sacrifices to the Great Asmodeus.

However, as a sign that his power is growing, our Lord has released the ravenous Piasa, the horned ones and the wild man of the mountains."

Pausing for a moment he surveyed the eager faces before him. They seemed as ready as they would ever be. Now to send them on their mission.

"The Master's creatures are even now abroad this night on a holy blood quest. They will be visiting those who live in the outlying farms to punish them for not worshipping the Master. They have desecrated his holy places, mocked him by the worship of their puny god in this valley. Now he has the right and power for his revenge. There will be much death this night to announce the Master's arrival.

"We of the Order of Asmodeus, in the meantime, have been assigned two important duties. First we must clear the interlopers form his Sanctuary and bring those in the town to be his eternal slaves. So go, my followers," he yelled with a broad sweep of his arms, "carry out our Master's will. Send those in town to meet our Master in death."

With a roar, the scarlet clad figures went streaming from the area, waving clubs and guns. They were filled with blood lust and were not to be denied. Death walked abroad in the stormy night.

Amanda Bennett thought she was certainly dead when that lunatic had pushed her into the hole. With her arms tied, she was unable to help herself or even grab for a handhold on the smooth sides of the shaft. As deep as the shaft appeared to be and as fast as she was falling, she knew that she would be smashed to bits when she hit the ground. Resigning herself to death, she closed her eyes and waited to die.

What she didn't see was that the shaft took a gentle turn and leveled out, so instead of hitting directly against the floor of the shaft, which would have killed her, she hit on a slope and rolled head over heels to the bottom. She wasn't killed, but she was mightily shaken up by the fall.

Finally, her mad tumble came to a stop. Bruised and sore, Amanda laid completely still, afraid to move and discover that her back or legs were broken. Her long hair was over her face and her only garment had worked its' way up around her neck leaving her naked body exposed, but she was alive.

Slowly her senses returned to normal. Discovering that nothing appeared to be broken, she struggled to move, tossing her head to move her long, thick hair from over her face. It seemed that the tunnel was not the pitch-blackness that she had expected, but was dimly lit by a peculiar green light.

Not willing to simply lay there and wait for something to find her, Amanda struggled to get to her feet, but found it almost impossible with her arms tied. Experimenting, she swung her body to try and regain her feet and brought herself to her knees. With a monumental effort, the woman forced herself to her feet and when she raised her head, found herself face to face with a true horror.

The creature was tall; well over her 5'9"" inch height, with an outer shell that looked like shiny metal. As unbelievable as the creature was, it was the face that drew and held her eyes. She felt that if evil had a face, this would be it. With something approaching a grin on its face, the thing reached out its human like hands to grasp Amanda by her slim waist. Battered, beaten, bruised and still bound, Amanda did what anyone would do in such a situation, she fainted.

CHAPTER TWENTY-ONE

The storm was raging ever stronger, covering the last resting place of Mace Runnels with a river of mud and debris as the upper road began to give way under the double onslaught of rain and wind. Soon no one would ever be able to find any sign of the fight that had taken place where Runnels had fallen.

Though the night was pitch black, not even the most complete and total darkness would completely mask the glow of the emerald gleam that pierced the darkness. An oval of emerald light came floating, in defiance of the hurricane force of the driving wind. The glow came to rest a few feet from Runnel's last resting place, to sit quietly for a long period of time.

As if it had been waiting for some signal that had now been received, the glowing emerald sphere began to pulsate slowly. Soon the pulsations became so rapid that the sphere began to glow brightly, until finally a ray of brilliant emerald light shot from the sphere to bath the battered body of Runnels in its light.

Though the Indian had made sure that his foe was dead before he left, after a few seconds of exposure to the beam of emerald light, the killer's battered body embedded in the mud began to twitch. With a convulsive twist, the killer raised his mud-covered face and gasped for breath, his head twisted at a peculiar angle. He slowly raised his left arm and wiped the thick, gooey mud from his bruised face, his vacant eyes gleamed as if lit from the inside.

"Human," called a soft voice, piercing the sounds of the storm as if it was a calm night.

"Who calls?" responded Runnels in what was almost a moan.

"Human, I am Hera. I speak for Asmodeus, the Prince of Evil."

The figure on the ground tried to get to his feet, but found that he couldn't move anything below the waist; he could only raise his head with great effort.

"I'm paralyzed; I can't feel my legs," gasped Runnels, "what happened to me?"

The emerald globe pulsated for a moment; the only sounds to be heard were the shriek of the wind and the driving rhythm of the rain.

"You are not paralyzed, human, you are dead." whispered the globe.

"If I'm dead, then how can I be talking to you," grunted Runnels, struggling to accept the fact that he was supposed to be dead but not dead.

"Asmodeus is the god of evil. He has need of servants who enjoy killing. On this night, Asmodeus begins to free himself from his eternal prison."

"What do you want from me?" gasped Runnels, beginning to feel the pain of his shattered ribs.

"Asmodeus offers you eternal life in return for eternal servitude." hummed the globe, the emerald beam bathing Runnels becoming broader and more intense. "All you must do is promise total servitude."

"Who's this Asmodeus guy?" grated Runnels, straining every muscle to lift himself from his muddy cradle.

"Asmodeus is the eternal lord of evil. He is all things to those who believe and support him. You are being offered the opportunity to live forever as a servant of the great lord Asmodeus."

His strength at an end, Runnels allowed himself to fall face down back into his muddy prison. Gasping for breath, Runnels raised is head one final time.

"What if I refuse? What happens to me then?"

The emerald globe made a sound that approximated laughter.

"Why, foolish mortal, if you don't agree to serve Asmodeus as one of his eternal servants, then you return to muck and mire from which your race came. This is your one and only chance to join with Asmodeus."

Runnels was beginning to shrug off the death like coldness that had numbed his brain from the moment the emerald light had awakened him from his slumbers. He began to realize that he was literally being forced to agree to serve this Asmodeus guy or die. It awoke his deep well of rage at being forced to do anything. He was Mace Runnels, he had almost succeeded in escaping from the country, only that Indian and this damn storm had stopped him.

Again that tinkling sound came from the emerald globe.

"You humans are so foolish. You think that your associates came to rescue you. They wait in the town below not to rescue you but to kill you. You would not have lasted an hour after arriving in that town."

"You lie!" spat Runnels, struggling again to raise himself from his belly. "They wouldn't do that. They need me. I'm too valuable to them."

The emerald globe pulsated again.

"You also know much more than they believe is good for them. Your friends have come to kill, not to rescue."

"I'll kill those bastards!" he yelled against the force and fury of the storm.

His hair trigger temper exploded and he strained every ounce of his being to get to his feet. Finally, he realized it was hopeless and accepted that he was a helpless cripple.

"You're barking up the wrong tree, whoever or whatever you are. I'm a helpless cripple; I think my back's broke."

Again he heard that silvery tinkling sound as the globe began to pulsate again.

"With the power of Asmodeus nothing is impossible. Accept and know his power."

What did he have to lose, thought the cripple?

"Fine! If you can cure me, then I'll work for your Asmodeus."

In answer the emerald glow again began to brighten until it light up the landscape as light as at midday. A low hum that Runnels had heard since regaining consciousness began that rise in volume until Runnels could feel it vibrating his very being. Soon his entire body was vibrating like a tuning fork. When it seemed to him that the sound could not get any higher in pitch, there was an intense flare of emerald light and both the light and sound vanished. Darkness again reigned supreme.

Shortly after Dr. Bonner had told his story, he had plead exhaustion and retired to his chosen bedchamber, formerly one of the old monks' cells. The rest had sat and talked for a while. The story had given them some idea of what was expected of them. Prior to this, they had believed that the project was an investigation into the uses of ESP for archeological and other type of searches. Even Dr. Peterson was intrigued enough to try and develop some hypothesis that would account for the interesting parts of Dr. Bonner's story.

"Of course," began Dr. Peterson, puffing on his ever present pipe, "The story could be a creation of a very sick mind. Bear in mind that there is no proof backing up his story. We only have Bonner's unsupported word to back up his unbelievable story.

"It is possible that Dr. Bonner has had a nervous breakdown and is actually suffering from delusions. He's obviously off in a world of his own and wants us in there with him."

Sheila had lost her temper at that point.

"Dr. Peterson, you are the most frustrating man I have ever met. When someone presents you with something that does not fall within the boundaries of your own little preconceived world, then you dismiss the one who presents the problem as deranged.

"It seems to me that you are merely trying to reassure yourself by down grading a great scientist. You haven't even bothered to investigate what he's said, but you are just dismissing it out of hand."

Dr. Peterson smiled condescendingly at her as he removed his pipe.

"My dear, you are but a beautiful child. When you have lived as long as I have, you will discover that this world runs based on a series of unchangeable scientific laws. What Dr. Bonner has told us, while a fascinating ghost story for children, cannot possibly be true. If it had been factual, then the many scientists assigned to the Manhattan Project would have surely investigated the situation thoroughly and gotten to the bottom of the situation. However, there has been no mention of this in any scientific journal. If it really happened at least one of two of those eminent scientists would have written a paper on the matter.

"Notice that instead of basing our project where the incident is supposed to have taken place, Monitoring Station 14, a mere mile or so up the summit of this mini-mountain, we are instead stuck here in this ancient rock heap talking about exploring the ether, whatever that is, and mental contact. No, child, it's clear, at least to me, that the "great man", as you call him, has had a mental breakdown. He believes in things that go bump in the night. Notice that very obvious hologram of the Indian that appeared so conveniently.

"No, my friends, I can't be a part of this. I'm leaving as soon as I can get packed. I suggest that the rest of you do the same."

So saying, Dr. Peterson rose and walked quickly from the Chapel. The rest silently watched him leave. Dr. Sonnerman shook his head slowly.

"This will be the end of Dr. Bonner's effectiveness in the scientific community. Peterson may be an insufferable ass, but he does have important connections in the scientific community. A word from Peterson into the wrong ears can ruin Bonner.

"I will submit that I cautioned Dr. Bonner about inviting Dr. Peterson to be a participant. While there is no question that Peterson is a brilliant scientist, he is always ready to tear down a competitor. Both he and Dr. Bonner were candidates for the 1987 Nobel Prize in physics. Dr. Bonner won. Peterson has never forgiven him."

Sheila stood and glared toward the door through which Peterson had left. With a shake of her lovely head she stretched and looked around.

"I'm going to bed," she said with a yawn. "You know, I never asked Dr. Bonner what he thought about the Indian. If it was a hologram as Dr. Peterson says, it was very effective, and I am still puzzled as to how he did it without any visible equipment."

"Not a hologram." came an unfamiliar voice, "but rather an old friend coming to give a warning of unspeakable evil."

They all swung around to see the black robed caretaker standing calmly just inside the door leading to the living quarters. His face still in the shadows of his cowl, the caretaker waited for their responses.

"My god, this is the first I've heard you speak." gasped Sheila.

"What do you know of this?" demanded Dr. Sonnerman.

"I know a great deal," responded the mysterious one, reaching up to throw back his cowl. "I am Randolph Santos. I have fought the evil that inhabits this place for over sixty years.

Sheila entered her cell and, dimming her "cot" side lamp, she began to unbutton her blouse. Her thoughts were running riot regarding the earlier discussion. If Randolph Santos were to be believed then this Mission and, in fact, the entire hill was the home to a living evil god. She was actually having trouble accepting the enormity of what the caretaker had told her. It was clear that they were living on borrowed time.

Added to the danger from the ancient god, there was also the threat to Dr. Bonner, a man who had been closer to her than her own father. She couldn't allow Dr. Peterson to harm Dr. Bonner's career. She had to think of something. She was so engrossed in her thoughts that it was only belatedly that she realized that she was no longer alone.

Whirling around, she clutched her blouse shut and backed against the wall, looking for a weapon. Standing between her and the door, was a man. No, it was an Indian. With total surprise, she finally noted that it was the solid version of the flickering figure that she had seen in the Chapel.

"Who are you?" she demanded in a quavering voice, "What do you want?"

The handsome Indian Warrior stood with his arms folded and calmly observed her with his dark, brooding eyes.

"My identity is not important. It is yours that concerns me." he said in a voice that seemed to come from far away, "He for whom I have waited for more of your years that you have seen lies hurt near here. You are the one to bring him here, to guide him, to care for him in your world. He is the only hope of you and yours surviving the day of evil."

His words were so puzzling that she almost forgot her fear as her scientific curiosity came to the fore.

"You can't be real. I mean you seem to appear at will. Are you a hologram?" she demanded.

"God, that was a stupid question," she scolded herself," If you are a hologram then you can't answer. You are part of a dream, or a hallucination. I've worked too hard and I'm asleep, dreaming you."

The figure before her smiled slightly.

"I am no dream as you understand it. I am a vision sent to warn you. You have very little time. It is imperative that you go to Him who is destined to be your mate in this carnation. He that was, is and will be lies injured near to the entrance to the road that leads to this place. You are the only one who can help him."

Sheila was tiring of the riddles and her own none to level temper was beginning to heat up.

"Listen, Cochise or whoever you might be. I don't have a mate, as you put it. I don't want a mate. I wouldn't know what to do with a mate. Besides, don't you know that this is the nineties, I don't have to go do anything, so if you will just fade away, or whatever it is that you spooks do, I intend to go to bed."

Shoulders slumped the Indian looked at her sadly.

"You do not believe, yet within your heart and soul you know what I say is true. You and only you can revive and save He who is, was and shall be. If you do not save him, then you and all in this valley will die painfully this night. The evil one has released his devil hounds. He desires the return of his home that you have desecrated. You, none of you, will see the morning light. I have failed."

With that final statement, the solid looking figure began to slowly fade from sight. The last thing she saw as he vanished was his very sad eyes. Suddenly, she recalled the story of Randolph Santos and realized the identity of the Indian.

"Old One, please wait!" she called, but it too late. In seconds Sheila was alone in her cell, with no sign that anyone other than she had ever been there.

With a sigh, she dropped down on her cot, her brow furrowed as she weighed her options. When the Indian had appeared in the Chapel, Dr. Peterson had accused Dr. Bonner of rigging a hologram projector. Dr. Bonner had not denied it, but then he had not been directly asked about the hologram by anyone other than Peterson. She was certain that Dr. Bonner had not, and would not; rig a hologram projector in her bedroom. It would have gained him nothing, since she fully believed in what he was doing. He had been her favorite professor in college and she had turned to him when she had disagreed with her own father. He wouldn't take advantage of her in this manner.

So, what if the Indian had really been in her room? But there was the wild story told earlier by the caretaker; if any of it was true then they were all in great danger.

He had told them of his mother and sister being killed at their hacienda by some type of creatures and his own battle with the flying monster at the Fuentes hacienda. He had held onto the neck of the flying beast as it had flown through the night carrying his beloved in its talons. The creature had finally been able to throw him off as it had approached Devil's Hill. He had crashed into heavy brush that had covered most of the slope of the hill, breaking several bones, but nothing life threatening. From his vantage point on the lower slope, he had watched the creature land somewhere near the summit of the hill.

Santos had tried to bull his way through the brush to follow the creature, but his injuries were too serious. He had limped to the Mission where the Monks had taken him in and nursed him back to health. In frenzy, he had searched every inch of Devil's Hill, but while he had found many strange tracks, he had not found any sign of his beloved.

At the altar in the Mission, he had sworn to dedicate is life to finding the missing woman and killing the creature. He had abandoned the outside world and taken a vow to remain in the Mission, forsaking the outside world. He had made only one contact with his former life, which was to send word to his father of his vow and his quest. His father had understood and helped him fake his own death. That had been sixty years ago. All that time he had lived in the Mission, uttering not a word, enforcing a personal vow of silence.

He had lain hidden and watched the slaughter of the Monks by the minions of the evil one. In the search of the buildings, by the demons, he had been missed. He had tried to follow the creatures back to their lair, but lost them in the darkness near the summit of Devil's Hill. All the evidence he could find always pointed toward the summit. The summit was also the location of Monitoring Station 14. There might actually be a serious connection.

Santos had identified the so-called hologram as an actual person. An old Indian called only the Old One. In spite of her natural skepticism, all the facts seemed to be pointing in the same direction. If that was true, then perhaps the rest of the information was true. If the vanishing Red Man was really the same Old One that had been a friend of Randolph Santos, then perhaps the story of someone injured that she needed to help was true.

What if someone was lying injured at the foot of the drive? What if that person died because she was too stubborn to listen to a vision? What if she was starting to crack up and Dr. Peterson was the only sane one in the place? There was only one way to find out.

Rising, she grabbed her black cloak, pulling it on as she ran lightly down the corridor. As the one who ran most of the errands for the group, she always had access to the truck. If nothing else, she thought, if she took the truck. Dr. Peterson would be unable to leave until she returned. That, in and of itself, would be a good thing in her estimation, as it would give the excitable physicist time to calm down.

Assured that no one was watching her, she pulled open the outer door, slipping through and pulling it tight behind her, to stagger back against the rough Mission wall as the full force of the storm struck her. Lowering her head, she staggered across the exposed courtyard to where they had parked the truck after returning from the trip to El Noche. Grabbing at the door handle to keep from being swept off her feet, Sheila wrenched the door open and pulled herself inside. She was absolutely drenched, her long crimson hair plastered to her head. The cloak plastered against her body.

She started the engine and drove carefully out of the courtyard. The force of the wind was such that she had to struggle to keep the truck pointed in the direction in which she wished to drive. She literally was forced to descend the drive inches at a time, riding the brakes of the old truck to keep from being blown off the road into the deep ditches on either side.

The end of the drive way where it joined the Devil's Hill cut off was only a mile from the Mission, but due to the lack of visibility, and the winding course of the drive way, it took her over a half an hour to reach that point. The Indian had said that the injured party was near the end of the drive, so she parked her truck in the brush at the edge of the road to rummage under the seat. Finally, she came up with a powerful flashlight. Pointing it at her face, she flicked the switch and was almost blinded by the high intensity beam of light. Satisfied, she took a tight hold on the flash and pushed against the driver's door with all her might. By exerting all of her strength she forced the door open just enough for her to fall through and land with a splash on the muddy ground.

Well, she thought, as she fought her way to her feet, I couldn't be more wet if I had taken a bath in my clothes, so what's a little more mud. Wiping her long wet hair from her face, she started to walk west along the cut off, having to fight for every step against what felt like a sold wall of wind and rain. There seemed to be no respite, the force of the wind actually seemed to be getting higher as she moved further away from the entrance to the Mission. Every hard won step depleted her energy to the point that she was literally exhausted before she had gone fifty feet. Finally, she decided to give up and go back. The Indian was some kind of sick joke at her expense, Peterson was right.

As she turned to retrace her steps, her light reflected off something against the hillside, mere feet in front of her. Gathering her remaining strength, Sheila Bennett fought her way over to the mud-covered object. To her great surprise, she found that it was a wrecked van.

Moving around the vehicle, she found that the nose was crumpled into the side of the hill. It was lying on its' left, or driver's side. The passenger window was shattered. She bent down and flashed her light inside.

"Hello?" she said tentatively.

Her only answer was the piercing wail of the terrible wind, the pounding of the rain on the metal vehicle and the mighty crash of thunder. Getting up her courage, she stuck her head partially into the van through the passenger window and looked for survivors. Her light showed that there were two figures inside. Taking care not to snag her cloak on the glass shards still in the window frame, Sheila gingerly crawled inside. Even if they were both dead, she reasoned, she would be sheltered from the elements for at least a few moments.

The first individual she reached, wearing some kind of uniform, was definitely dead. His skin was ice cold to the touch and a small round hole in the right side of his head, revealed by her flashlight, showed that he had been shot. As if that wasn't enough to convince her that he was dead, the dried brains plastered on the inside of the window would have been sufficient proof. Making the sign of the cross, Sheila grabbed a wadded up shirt nearby and reverently draped it over the dead man's face.

Crawling further back into the wrecked vehicle, pushing her light before her, Sheila felt for the second man's throat. To her surprise, she felt a faint pulse. He was still alive. Using her light, she determined that didn't appear to have any broken bones, but she did find a lump on the side of his head. She also noted that he was wearing a prison uniform. Great, she thought, I come out in this hell to rescue a convict. Wonder where this Other is, she thought as she twisted the man's head to check for other wounds.

A movement at the rear of the passenger compartment caused her to sit up and flood the area with her light. Sitting cross-legged against the far wall was the Indian that had appeared in her room.

"What are you doing here?" she demanded, giving him her powerful light full in his face.

The Indian who looked older in the glaring light than he had in her chamber never moved his eyes from the unconscious man on the floor.

"As it was ordained by the Great Spirit long ago, I watch over the only one who can defeat the evil one," he said softly, "He is the Other who must be protected until he can once again fight the evil one."

Sheila snorted as she turned the light back on the unconscious convict.

"Your Other is a convict, a criminal. You brought me out in this storm for a common criminal. I don't believe it. I could have been killed for nothing."

The Indian shook his head slowly, his eyes never leaving the unconscious figure.

"No, he is not criminal. No force or tribunal had pronounced him guilty of any crime. He is one of the greatest heroes that ever walked this land. He had a great loss of someone very dear to him, a loss he couldn't live with because he still feels that he could have saved her. In his grief he pronounced himself as guilty of her death and selected the only punishment that he could. He decided to imprison himself as a self-punishment.

"He imprisoned himself in his ancient home. In widening the prison, his ancient home was discovered and he was found. His appearance is similar to that of a prisoner that escaped decades ago and he was taken into custody for his identify to be determined.

"The Ancient Gods of this land still live, though they have given way to the current God of the Christians. The Great Spirit understood his grief and left him alone in his solitude. But now even the Gods fear the evil one and need for their champion to return to once again defeat the Master of Evil."

Sheila shook her head in frustration.

"Listen, bud, I have no idea what you are talking about, but I do know one thing, this man appears to have a concussion, he could die. In fact, if we don't get him to the Mission he will die."

Again the Indian smiled that small smile and shook his head.

"No little one. The Other may not die, his curse is to live. But he should and must live as himself, not as this shell of the man he once was."

Sheila looked askance at the Indian and sniffed.

"Little one, my ass! Listen Chief if you want me to help him, you have to help me get him to my truck. The wind's so high I'll never be able to carry him by myself."

Sadly, the Indian looked at her helplessly.

"Alas, I cannot do as you ask. It is forbidden for me to touch the Other. To do so would mean my death. I am only a Watcher. A Watcher may not touch a living God, but only watch and try to guide."

He paused and his dark eyes turned to the outside. She followed his glance and thought she saw some movement at the front of the van. Something else was walking about in the night.

"It is too late." he said, "The evil one has found the Other. May the Gods of both your and my people help us."

CHAPTER TWENTY-TWO

Sheriff Stark was making a monumental effort to keep his patrol car on the road and his mind on his job, but the weather was making it almost impossible for him to even see where he was going. Suddenly, he slammed on his brakes and skidded several feet. As he had feared, part of the Devil's Hill cut off was blocked by a mudslide. The only other way out of the valley was impassible.

Benji Marsters sat listless against the passenger door, his eyes staring vacantly into the night. Stark had to admit that the boy had received quite a shock, enough to send anyone off the deep end. Actually, for fourteen, Stark thought the boy was handling the matter very well. Since leaving his Uncle's ranch, the boy had not spoken. Stark glanced over at him as he heard the boy stir.

"What could have done such a thing, Sheriff?"

Stark shook his head slowly, as he surveyed the mound of mud and debris that blocked the narrow road.

"Don't know son. It took some type of power to rip those barn doors from their hinges and toss them across the barnyard. I ain't never seen no tracks like those in the barn either. But don't you worry, we'll find whoever did this and make them pay."

The scene had been even more gruesome than Benji had described. Old Zeke had been literally crushed by something far more powerful than a man. His face had been almost ripped off his head. The area around the barn had been literally awash with blood, both human and animal.

Stark was a brave man, but he was also a prudent man. Riot gun in hand, Stark, with Benji close behind, had edged his way into the partially destroyed barn. In the beam of his light, the results of Zeke Marsters' losing battle could be easily seen. It was also clear that the sturdy cow pen inside the barn had been destroyed by something.

"Baby's gone." Benji had offered.

"Baby?" questioned Stark, his eyes probing the deep shadows.

"Uncle Zeke's prize bull." answered the boy in a trembling voice, "He always kept Baby in that pen."

They hadn't found a living thing on the farm.

"Sheriff, you out there?" came a voice over his radio, interrupting his dark thoughts.

Stark had begun the laborious process of turning around, but unable to control the car with just one hand, Stark braked and grabbed his microphone. He was actually glad for the interruption; he really didn't want to continue the discussion with the boy.

"This is the sheriff." he responded.

"Sheriff, this is Jimmy. I'm over at the McNabb farm northeast of town. I can't find anyone around, but I caught sight of something big running across the yard when I came down the road. I think that this is a serious situation that is gonna require your attention."

Jimmy Squires was his only deputy, a big, confident, quiet man. If Jimmy Squires couldn't handle the matter himself, then it had to be serious.

"What's the problem, Jimmy?" asked the Sheriff.

The only response that Stark received was a burst of static, as there came another crash of thunder and bolt of lightning. He keyed his microphone again.

"Jimmy, this is the Sheriff, what's the problem?"

Again, no answer came.

"Jimmy, do you hear me?"

Static was his only answer. With an oath, Stark tossed the microphone back on the seat and took a firm grip on the wheel with both hands.

"Hang on, Kid." Stark said as he floored the accelerator.

Stark was far more concerned than he wanted Benji to know. Something was definitely wrong, or Jimmy would have responded. Of all the people he had hired as a deputy since first being elected Sheriff, Jimmy was the most dependable. Jimmy Squires was well able to handle anything that could possibly arrive. Stark was heading for the McNabb place as fast as the weather would allow.

It was a wild roller coaster ride of a drive even at fifteen miles an hour, but Stark finally arrived at the McNabb Farm. Benji Marsters hadn't said a single word during the entire trip.

Silas McNabb was a crusty old sole with a long-suffering wife and three gorgeous daughters of marriage age. The old man was so concerned that the local young bloods were continually planning to kidnap and rape his daughters that he kept them virtual prisoners in their own home and he even went so far as to usually do his chores with a shotgun handy. More than once, Stark had been forced to disarm old Silas before he had shot some young man just wanting to do some courting. It definitely interfered with the daughters dating.

The powerful cruiser fishtailed as he made the turn into the farmyard. Braking, he slid to a stop beside Jimmy's cruiser. The headlights of the other car were still on and the driver's door open. Grabbing his big flash from the seat, the Sheriff bulled open the driver's door.

"Whatever happens here kid, don't got out of this car," he ordered.

Without waiting for an answer Stark slogged his way across to the other police car and noted that the shotgun was gone from the inside rack. Turning, he felt something crunch beneath his feet in the mud and reached down to pick up Jimmy's microphone, ripped from the police radio. Flashing his light around, he also noticed several expended shotgun shells littering the ground. He stooped and picked up one, to see that it was double ought buck and the same brand he had issued to Jimmy.

Being cautious by nature, Ben Stark quickly returned to his own car to once again remove his riot shotgun from the inside rack. Benji had dropped down to the floorboard. Opening the trunk, he filled his pockets with spare shells. A veteran of the Vietnam War and numerous other conflicts, Ben Stark was always prepared. He was also a man that listened to his inner voice, which at the moment was screaming like a banshee. Something was very wrong at the McNabb home.

Slamming the car trunk, Stark flicked off his flashlight and stuck it in the pocket of his raincoat. No point in giving anyone hiding in the darkness a lit target to shoot at, he thought to himself. Crouching down, he ran as well as he could in the mud and rain to flatten himself against the west wall of the house, riot gun held at port arms. So far he couldn't see anything, but his sixth sense said that there was something wrong.

As carefully as possible, he slid along the side of the house toward the side door. He had visited the McNabb house several times since he had been elected sheriff and knew that the side door gave direct access to the kitchen. He'd rather enter through the back than go charging in the front.

It seemed like the trip to the rear door took forever, but soon, Stark was crouched to the left side of the screen door, or rather where the screen door would have been if it was still attached to the house. Not only was the screen door gone, but also the inner solid wooden door was splintered and lying on the floor, ripped from its hinges. The small porch that led to the kitchen door was empty. He could see that the kitchen door had also been ripped open.

As Stark was preparing himself to dart inside, an unusually violent crash of lightning illuminated the farmyard as bright as daylight. From the corner of his eye, Stark noticed what appeared to be a form lying on its back on the ground, arms out flung. Slowly, he surveyed the area, half expecting to see something out of the ordinary.

Seeing no movement, Stark darted over to the still form and, with a sinking heart, recognized the uniform as being that of Jimmy Squires. The uniform was all that he could use to identify the young deputy for his head was gone; it had been ripped from his shoulders. Lying in the mud near the body was his Jimmy's riot shotgun. The barrel of the shotgun was bent almost double. His sidearm was nowhere to be seen. It was clear that he had died facing his killer, but there was no sign of anyone or anything else in the yard.

Backing away from the horror before him, Stark regained his feet and, chambering a round, slogged back to the house. Just as he reached the corner of the house a blinding flash of lightning illuminated the yard as if it was daylight. The brightness was penetrating in its intenseness, Stark's night vision was totally destroyed, and he was effectively blind.

Crouching for a moment at the near edge of the open rear door, he waited for his eyes to readjust to the darkness before darting quickly inside the outer porch. He made it as quietly as possible across the porch to crouch by the destroyed kitchen door. Straining his eyes and ears, Stark tried to determine if there was anything in the kitchen. He heard nothing.

Left with no choice, moving very slowly, but with his shotgun ready, the Sheriff peered around the doorframe and scanned the empty kitchen. Taking a deep breath, Stark almost flowed through the doorway and placing his booted feet carefully, crossed the kitchen. His eyes missed nothing, it was clear that a violent battle had taken place in that previously cheerful room. The refrigerator was partially lying against the counter, chairs were broken and the kitchen table was lying on its side.

Reaching the other side of the kitchen, Stark slowly dropped to his knees to crouch beside the entry way into the living room. He could see nothing moving in the darkness of the room. The house was silent.

Deciding to take a chance, Stark pulled his light and flicked it on, the wide beam flooding the room with light. It looked like a mad house inside, the furniture was smashed and there was blood everywhere. He could see a pair of legs sticking out from beneath the overturned couch. Cautiously, Stark pulled the couch back over onto its legs and saw that the legs belonged to Silas McNabb, whose body was lying on the floor. He winced at the sight of the terrible wound in the old man's chest. It looked like someone had taken a chain saw to him.

For just a second, the wind lessened and Stark's ears caught a muffled sound from the bedroom area. It sounded like grunting to him. Flicking off his light, Stark silently made his way across the littered room and down the short hall. The sounds seemed to be coming from the first room on the left. Probably a bedroom, thought Stark, trying to remember the layout of the house. The door was partially shut.

"No--- no---." came a repetitive moan from the darkened room. "Please, no more."

Gathering his courage, Stark lifted his left foot and kicked the door open, flicked on his flashlight and stepped into the doorway, shotgun at the ready. On the bed was a woman whose clothes had been almost ripped from her slim body. There was blood on her face, which could be seen over the shoulder of the figure lying on top of her. Her eyes were wide, staring up as she moaned piteously. When the form between her legs turned to glare at him, Stark could see that while the creature was relatively human in form, one look at its' face showed that it was anything but human.

In one rapid move, the creature spun away from his victim to stand, fully erect at the foot of the bed, glaring at the intruder. Stark could see that the creature was big, taller than Ben's six foot two inch frame and much broader. What skin could be seen was dark red, covered by long shaggy hair. Disturbed in the act of having his way with Janet McNabb, old Silas' oldest daughter, the creature sprang at the Sheriff, raising its' muscular arms and roaring with a force that literally shook the walls. It was one pissed off monster.

The sight of the creature paralyzed Ben's conscious mind, but luckily for him, his trigger finger had a mind of its' own. Firing so rapidly that it sounded like one shot, Ben triggered three rounds of buck shot at the creature, the majority of the lead pellets catching the thing in the upper chest. The monster was blown off its' feet, tumbling across the bed to slam into the far wall.

Like a dog shaking off water, the thing got back to its' feet and roared its battle cry again. Taking careful aim, Ben fired the last two shells in the magazine directly into the monster's face even as it leapt at him. His claw-like hands over his shattered face, the creature missed its target and crashed to the floor. Stark back pedaled out of the creature's reach, loading his shotgun as fast as he could move his fingers.

Moving slower, but still rapidly by Stark's calculations, the creature regained its feet and threw itself through the window, taking out both the glass and the sash as he fled. Wailing like a banshee, the creature loped off into the night.

Thumbing more shells into the shotgun, Ben ran over to the window and fired at the running figure, periodically illuminated by the flashes of lightning. He felt a great satisfaction when he knocked it from its' feet again. To his shock and amazement, the thing got back to its' feet again, appearing none the worse for wear, and disappeared into the night. Only the dead deputy and the rain were left in the farmyard.

Moving slowly away from the window so as to not be seen from the outside, Stark turned back to the woman on the bed. She appeared to have passed out. He shook her shoulder.

"Janet!" he said urgently, "Janet, we've got to get out of here!"

He received no response, so he shook her again. She was totally limp, her skin clammy to the touch. Struck by a horrible suspicion, he placed his left hand on her throat, feeling for a pulse in her neck with his thumb, he found none. Flicking on his light, Stark flashed it over the dead woman looking for a wound. He found none until he illuminated the area between her widely spread legs. The sheets in that area were totally soaked with dark blood. It was clear that the creature had literally ripped her open in its attempt to have its way with her.

Swallowing the bile that filled his throat, Ben Stark slowly pulled the bloody sheet over her dead white face and left the room of death. Pausing in the doorway to flick off his light and give his eyes time to adjust to the darkness. Slowly, cautiously, he moved further down the hallway, into the bedroom area. Some sixth sense told Stark that there were other living creatures in the house.

In the next room, obviously the master bedroom, he found Silas' wife, Mamie McNabb, lying in a bathtub of bloody water. Her arms hung limply over the edge of the tub, her dead eyes open and staring, above her mangled throat. Her blank eyes stared up at him, a look of horror frozen for all eternity on her dead face.

Backing out of the room, Stark started back across the bedroom but froze in his tracks when he heard a faint sound come from the closet. With the barrel of his weapon, Stark eased opening the door of the closet very slowly. Flicking on his light, he at first saw only a rack of clothes and a row of women's shoes. He didn't see anything, but he knew that he had heard a sound coming from the closet.

As Stark began to slowly back out of the closet, his light showed a figure crouched down in the far corner, partially covered behind hanging garments. Slowly, he leaned forward and pulled the clothes aside revealing the figure more clearly. He relaxed slightly when he saw it was a fully human female. It took him a moment to realize it, but he was looking at Betty McNabb, at 24, Silas and Mamie McNabb's youngest daughter.

Dropping to one knee, he placed a hand on Betty's quivering shoulder.

"Betty," he said gently, "Betty, its Ben Stark. Remember me, I'm the sheriff."

Slowly, she turned her head away from the wall to look directly at him. Her face was contorted as if she had lost her reason.

"Sh---Sheriff?" she looked at him as if she couldn't believe that he was real. Slowly, she reached out one tiny hand and touched his face. When she was assured that he was actually there and not a dream, she threw himself into his big arms.

"Oh, God Sheriff. It was horrible. Those things came pouring into the house, roaring and breaking things. I saw them kill---- my father. He's dead." she said, her voice muffled by his chest.

Stark patted her back softly and held her tightly, swiveling to keep is eyes on the dark room behind him.

"It's O.K. now, my dear. I'm gonna get you back to town and everything will be fine. Come on now; let me get you out of this closet. We need to get going before those things come back. Do you understand me, Betty?"

Nodding slowly, she let him help her stumble out of the closet. Taking her hand, he placed her fingers around his pistol belt.

"I need both hands free in case they come back, so you keep a tight hold on my belt. I don't want to lose you in the dark. We've got to get out of here."

"I understand, Sheriff. You lead and I'll follow. You—you don't think they'll come back, do you?" she quavered.

"I don't know, honey. But we're getting out of here just in case."

Slowly, the Sheriff started back down the hall, his light illuminating the area around him as he moved. Betty shuffled slowly along behind him. He could feel that she had a death grip on his belt. He sincerely hoped that he didn't have to run. He'd have to carry her.

He checked the other two bedrooms before starting back for the front. While he said nothing to Betty McNabb, he was very concerned that he couldn't find the third McNabb daughter, Carla. He didn't want to think of her being carried off by the creatures. Ordinarily, he would have followed after the thing he had shot, to insure that it was dead. Unfortunately, with Betty McNabb being a big responsibility, he decided that the best thing to do was get back to town and raise a search party.

Taking her small hand in his, Stark led her across the devastated living room, being careful not to go near her father's body. He stopped to the side of the front door. Slowly, he turned the knob, eased open the door and peered outside. Due to the storm and the driving rain he couldn't see anything. He turned toward the girl cringing at his side.

"Betty, when I say now, we are going to run for my car. Then we are heading for town. Do you understand?"

She nodded timidly.

Ben Stark smiled down at her, even terrified, she was a beauty.

"O.K., let's go."

Bolting from the front door, the two were almost knocked from their feet by the force of the storm. Clinging to each other, they fought their way across the farmyard to his waiting patrol car. Stark forced open the driver's door and allowed the girl to slide across the seat. He reached across her to lean his riot gun against the far door. He noticed that Benji was wedged into a small ball under the dash. Slowly, Stark crawled behind the wheel with a sigh of relief. He couldn't believe how tired he was.

With a smile, he reached forward to report to dispatch. His hand closed on air. Glancing down, he saw that the microphone had been ripped from his radio. Straightening up, his eyes sought the rearview mirror and found that he was staring into the eyes of one of the creatures. It was in the car. Desperately, he grabbed for his sidearm, but the creature roared and grabbed Stark by the head.

The creature's strength was enormous. Stark was a powerful man, himself, but he was like a baby as it began to slam Stark's head against the driver's door. He felt his consciousness slipping away as he clawed for his sidearm. Each time he grabbed for his pistol, the creature would slam his head even harder against the door.

Finally, in an unbelievable display of physical strength, Stark managed to pull his .44, but when he tried to raise it the creature knocked it out of his hand. As the world began to go lack for Ben Stark the last sound he heard was Betty McNabb screaming hysterically.

Dr. Peterson was beside himself with rage. Leave it to that Bennett slut to screw everything up, he thought. She had disappeared into the night with the only transportation available. He kicked his bags childishly. How dare that scheming bitch plot against him? Now he was stuck here.

For the fifth time in as many minutes, he tore open the outer door and walked outside to look about for Sheila Bennett's return. With an oath he turned to stomp back into the building. As he reached for the door, there was a sound behind him, but before he could turn, something went around his neck.

Surprised, he raised his hands to grip the wire that was around his neck. He could feel the pressure increasing as he fought for breath. He tried to yell for help, but over the sound of the raging storm, he knew that no one could hear him. The wire was so tight that it was difficult for him to make a sound, as he silently struggled to free himself.

As the struggled, his attacker pulled him away from the sanctuary represented by the closed door to the Monastery, so close and yet so far. He was seeing stars before his eyes as he was pulled to the ground. With a final shutter, he died.

The scarlet robed figure that had killed Dr. Peterson gently opened the door and peered inside, he saw nothing. Turning, he waved to his compatriots waiting across the courtyard. As they came running silently across the rain slick courtyard, he held the door while they entered one at a time. They spread out and silently filtered through building.

CHAPTER TWENTY-THREE

Sheila Bennett crouched by the unconscious prisoner and peered out through the window trying to see what the Indian had spotted outside the van. All she could see was rain and darkness.

"What did you see?" she whispered.

"Death." answered the Indian, his head turning as if he was following the progress of something moving outside the van.

Beginning to feel a twinge of fear, Sheila shook the unconscious convict.

"Hey you, wake up," she urged as she shook him again. "We gotta get out of here."

Romar watched as his father battled the Prince of Evil. Finally, in a display of power that stunned even him, Romar was amazed to see that Asmodeus was hurled to the ground to crash in the field before him. With a roar, Roar raced toward the fallen creature and placed his sword against its throat. Slowly, Asmodeus opened his eyes and turned the power of his gaze fully on Romar. He felt as if he stood in the open door to a blast furnace, such was the power of Asmodeus' gaze.

Though his attention was fully captured by Asmodeus, Romar was still aware of the danger that threatened him. Breaking away from the power of Asmodeus' gaze, Romar found himself facing the black clad one he had seen standing beside Asmodeus on the wall.

Leaping from the prostrate evil one, Romar raised his sword to block the wild swings of his opponent. The battle was short, but deadly. Finally, Romar disarmed his foe and smashed him to the ground with a blow with the side of his blade.

His vanquished for looked at him for a long moment then raised one hand to make a sign upon the air.

"There will be another time and another place. Kinsman."

With that the black-garbed stranger faded from sight.

Romar turned to see the Great Anu standing regally over the fallen Asmodeus. Glowing bonds of force held Asmodeus in nuclear bondage.

"Asmodeus," said Anu in a voice like thunder. "You have conspired against the throne. For that you are banished for all eternity to a rocky prison in the farthest reaches of the empire. What say you?"

"I will have my revenge, traitor,' snarled Asmodeus. "I should rule and not you. You killed our father and stole his throne."

Anu shook his mighty head in despair. The old wrong was still haunting his world and would for all eternity. With an imperious wave of his hand, Anu gave a command and the very air around Asmodeus began to turn dark and soon the evil one was sealed within a block of dark matter. Anu turned to those around him.

"Michael."

"Sire." responded his Champion.

"Take this thing to the western reaches of our empire and bury it in the earth as far as possible."

"At once, Lord."

Immediately, Michael and a squad of his guard loaded the encase figure of Asmodeus in a flyer and left for the west. Anu looked at his son with pride.

"You faced Asmodeus and did not flinch. No one has ever done that. I am proud of you my son."

Before Romar could say anything, they were joined by Amazonia.

"Lord, what of the creatures?" she asked indicating those nightmarish creatures who still scampered about the field.

"They are, or were, followers of Asmodeus changed by the magic released by Athena and her son. In their own way they are also immortal, so a certain extent."

"Lord-beware!" came a scream.

The three turned to see the lady Athena appearing a short distance away. In her hands she held a nuclear particular beam weapon, as deadly to the Gods as to a human. As she fired, Anu stepped in front of his wife and son, taking the full brunt of the beam himself. In seconds it fused his armor and sapped his strength. He fell to the ground.

As the mighty Anu crumpled to his knees, Romar drew and threw his dagger at Athena's legs, knocking her to her knees. The weapon fell from her hands.

Amazonia and Romar dropped to their knees beside the stricken Supreme God while bodyguards swarmed over the Lady Athena.

"My Lord." Said Amazonia softly, cradling his massive head on her lap.

Anu opened his eyes and gazed fondly at his wife.

"I have not left on the trip to the nether reaches just yet, my wife."

Romar jumped to his feet and took command.

"Summon the Royal Physician."

He paused and looked directly at the evil she-devil that had done such harm.

"Hold that creature for the Lord Anu's pleasure." He commanded the guard.

To her complete surprise, her touch seemed to work a miracle. With a moan, the man twitched and tried to roll over. Straining under his weight, she helped him move back against the seat. He moaned again as he raised his big hands to rub his face.

"Wh---wh---what happened?" he asked in a hoarse croak, as if his voice hadn't been used in a long time.

"You were in a wreck." she said, "You've got a big bump on the side of your head. But that's not important right now, mister. Right now we have to get away from whatever is out there."

He raised his head and looked at her, it was clear that he was having trouble focusing his eyes. Suddenly, to her shock, his face lit up and his eyes began to blaze as he grabbed her arms tightly in his big hands.

"Marie, you've come back to me. I thought I'd lost you, but you didn't die, you're back. They said you were dead. I tried, my darling, but I couldn't get to you."

Startled, she pushed away from him.

"Hold it mister! I'm not your Marie. My name is Sheila Bennett."

"But you look just like ------." his face fell. "You're not Marie Rogelio?"

She solemnly shook her head.

"No, I am not. I am not this Marie person, I told you that I am Sheila Bennett."

His face fell as if an internal light had been switched off. A sound from the direction of the broken passenger window recalled her to the danger.

"The Indian says that there's something outside."

He looked up at her with a puzzled expression.

"What Indian?" he asked softly.

She pointed behind him.

"That one ----- why where did he go?" she said as she frantically searched the interior with her eyes. "He was here a minute ago. Honestly. He said he was sent to watch over you."

The stranger got to his knees and crawled toward the front of the vehicle. At a loss for what to do, Sheila decided the best thing to do was follow him. She joined him as he crouched by the open window.

"What's the matter?" she asked quietly.

"I smell something that I don't like," he said, his piercing eyes scanning the night.

He started to move forward, but she stopped him with a small hand on his arm.

"Before we start, at least tell me your name."

He hesitated for a long moment and then shook his head.

"I can't, I don't remember, ma'am."

"But you could remember this Marie girl. Surely you can remember your own name."

He smiled slowly, "You can call me whatever you desire.

Suddenly he tensed, his dark piercing eyes probing the darkness.

"Be very, very quiet."

At the look on his face, she froze. Before her startled eyes, he seemed to ooze out from under her hand and disappear through the broken window into the darkness, leaving her crouched by the opening. She had never felt so alone, during those few minutes that the big man was gone. As silently as he had vanished, he came to the opening and reached out his hand to her.

"We need to go quickly. I killed that one, but there are more here."

"Killed what?" she yelled over the rain as she allowed him to help her to her feet.

He favored her with a long look.

"A creature of the night!"

Holding her close, the big man led her through the rain, paying no attention that she could see to the storm that raged around them. He might as well have been out for a stroll on a balmy night for all the attention he paid to the storm. He was unlike anyone she had ever known, she thought, as she pointed the way to where she had left the truck.

Nick Martony was getting more uneasy by the moment. Like most killers, he had a sixth sense regarding his own personal safety. Something was wrong, seriously wrong, he felt, but he couldn't determine what was wrong. All he could do was sit and watch the situation develop.

Molena seemed very content to wait out the storm. It was now evident that something had delayed Runnels. It was just as evident that they were stuck here for the duration. The ability to sit patiently when others felt the need to move had gained Molena a criminal empire so he could afford to sit patiently in such comfortable surroundings.

Over the sounds of the storm came a pounding on the front door. Petey roused himself from dozing by the fire and stumbled over to the door. Bracing the door to keep it from ripping from its' hinges, he unlocked the latch. A small, muddy figure came walking calmly through the door. Martony tensed when he was that the new arrival was the long awaited Runnels.

Petey struggled to close the door, but the force of the wind was such that he was unable to force it completely shut. Runnels reached over and, with one hand, gently closed the door. Petey looked at the newcomer in total surprise.

"God damn, Mister, you gotta be some kind of strong to be able to just shut this door. That wind hitting it has to be upwards of eighty miles an hour."

Mace Runnels smiled slowly, showing little emotion.

"Just leverage. You actually did most of the work."

Suddenly, remembering his manners, Petey walked over to the bar and poured a large mug of coffee from the ever-present pot and presented it to the soaking wet newcomer.

"On the house my friend. Someone as strong as you, I treat very politely."

Runnels accepted the coffee with a smile and took a deep drink. Over the rim of the mug, he slowly and carefully scanned the room. His gaze froze when he spotted Molena and Martony sitting quietly in the shadows beside the fireplace. Nodding his thanks to Petey, he walked slowly over to join the two mobsters.

"Mace, good to see you." said Molena offering the killer his hand.

Runnels calmly seated himself, placing his mug on the table ignoring the outstretched hand.

"Carlos, Nick, good to see you." he responded coolly.

"We was worried, Mace." offered Nick Martony, "What kept you?"

Mace favored him with a slight smile.

"A little weather problem; but that's all settled now."

Molena glanced back toward the door, a puzzled look on his face.

"You alone? Where's the Fed and the driver? We need to take care of them."

Runnels shrugged as he took another sip of his coffee.

"The Fed left us along the way and the driver was killed when the van was blown off the road by the storm," he remarked as if discussing some commonplace matter of no importance, "so I'm afraid it's just me."

Leaning back in his chair, Runnels glanced around the shadowy room. The majority of the others in the room were intent on their on matters. Petey was back behind the bar, urging another pot of coffee to a boil on his camp stove.

"Nice comfortable room." Runnels remarked. "Good place to get this farce over with."

"Farce?" questioned Molena, glancing quickly at Martony.

Runnels looked directly at him for the first time.

"Carlos, I know that the Council sent you to kill me. I also know that this entire jailbreak was staged just to get me out so that you could silence me. It really might have worked."

"Mace, how could you believe such a thing?" protested Molena,"we came to rescue you."

Seeing no point in waiting, Nick "Fingers" Martony's automatic appeared in his big right hand, pointed at Runnels. However, before Martony could pull the trigger, Runnels' own left hand had snatched the gun from his hand at blinding speed. Both mobsters simply gapped at the speed displayed by the killer. Runnels carelessly tossed the gun on the table.

Recovering from his surprise, Molena snapped his fingers.

"Tiny Joe, kill him."

From the deep shadows beside the fireplace, the massive bodyguard lumbered toward the slightly built killer, his ham like hands outstretched. Runnels never moved a muscle, but let the bigger man lift him from the chair. Suddenly, Runnels moved and it was the bodyguard who spun across the room to crash into a table, scattering its occupants.

Martony swung a hard right at Runnels, but his fist was caught in midair by Runnels' right hand. Jerking Martony's arm toward him, runnels slammed his left forearm into Martony's elbow. The sharp crack of the arm breaking and Martony's shriek of pain could be heard even over the storm.

Spinning to his right, Runnels backhanded Molena, sending him rolling across the room. Seeing his boss down, Tiny Joe let out a roar like a bull elephant and charged the little man. Like a bullfighter, Runnels waited to the last possible second before spinning aside to let the big man slam harmlessly into the wall.

Wasting not a second, Runnels moved in behind the bigger man and slammed his fists into his foe's kidneys, sending him to his knees. Wrapping both of his hands around Tiny Joe's baldhead, Runnels pulled him back and then with all of his power rammed the semi-conscious man's head into the sturdy wooden wall. Tiny Joe fell over backward, to sprawl limply on the stained floor.

Not even breathing hard after his exertions, Runnels walked slowly the length of the room to stand over the fallen, bloody Carlos Molena. His confidence shaken at seeing how easily Runnels had dispatched the huge bodyguard, Molena propelled himself backward with his hands, angling for the door.

"Mace, you got it all wrong," babbled the Mafia chieftain, "I never meant for nobody to do anything to you. You and me we always been pals. We came to rescue you, to help you get out of the country"

Runnels smiled slowly as he followed the crawling mobster.

"Sorry, Carlos, but I got a better offer."

"Is it money you want, Mace? Somebody on the council pay you to off me? Is that it? I'll double whatever you been offered. No, I'll triple it. Just don't hurt me," pleaded the terrified mobster, raising one hand as if to ward off the advancing killer.

"Sorry, but my new employer has offered me much more than mere money, Carlos. He's given me real power."

In his intensity to extract vengeance from Molena, Runnels had forgotten about Martony, who was down, but not out. The sound of two shots rang out and Runnels stumbled forward.

"Die, you bastard!" sneered Molena, getting to his feet and straightening his expensive suit coat. "I'll see you in hell, you two bit punk."

Runnels turned around to see Martony, right arm limp at his side, kneeling by the overturned table, his automatic clutched awkwardly in his left hand. Slowly, Runnels reached his right hand behind him to feel of his lower back. He brought his closed fist around to his front, palm up and held it out in front of him. His calm smile on his face, Runnels opened his fist and tilted his hand to allow two spent, crumpled lead bullets fell to the floor.

Mouth hanging open in shock, Martony fired twice more at the smiling face before him. Gaping wounds appeared on Runnels' smooth featured face, but almost immediately closed, as if they had never been. With a small shake of his head, Runnels turned back to Molena.

"Two bit punk?" he questioned as he advanced toward the mobster.

Spinning, the terror stricken mobster turned and ran for the door. Runnels knelt down and picked a splintered chair leg from the floor. Drawing back, he threw the wooden dowel like a javelin; it hit Molena in the center of his broad back, pinning him to the wall beside the door. Runnels walked over and satisfied himself that the mobster was dead.

Turning from his victim, Runnels walked back across the room to kneel beside Martony who was in a total state of mental collapse. Reaching down, Runnels took Martony's left hand, which still clutched the automatic, in his own, gently raising the hand until the barrel of the weapon was pointed at Martony's left temple. With no sign of emotion on is face; Runnels pressed the trigger, blowing the back of Martony's head across the room. He released his hold on the mobster to allow him to crumple to the floor before the fire.

Runnels got to his feet and turned around, to find that the dozen or so people in the room were lined up against the bar, staring at him in abject fear. The fight had only taken two or three minutes, so no one really had time to react. Petey was the first to gather his wits; he came running around the bar, a meat cleaver clutched in one hand.

"I don't know or care who are you mister, but no one spills blood in my place."

Runnels favored him with a faint smile.

"I have no quarrel with you, cook. These, who were supposed to be my friends, would have killed me had I not killed them."

"I don't care what your argument was with those guys, but you're leaving here now," snapped the enraged cook as he grabbed Runnels by the arm.

In another display of his blinding speed, Runnels grabbed the hand that held the meat cleaver. Effortlessly, Runnels overpowered the cook and forced him to slam the cleaver into his own chest. Petey flew back to land on his back with a thud, the front of his apron covered with blood.

Runnels walked slowly forward to the counter and poured himself another mug of coffee. He surveyed the others over the rim of the mug.

"I suggest we all sit down while we wait." he suggested with a smile.

"Wait?" asked Minnie Foster diffidently, "for who?"

"The Prince of Darkness."

CHAPTER TWENTY-FOUR

Ben Stark was first aware that his head hurt. Slowly, he raised his right hand to feel his head, but instead of skin and hair, he felt smooth cloth. Opening his eyes, he found that he was lying on a pile of hay. Slowly, turning his head Stark realized that he was in the barn; he could hear the pounding of the rain on the metal roof. He became aware that there was someone else close to him. He could hear the other person breathing.

He tried to sit up, but his head throbbed so bad that he only moaned and fell back. He felt someone move beside him.

"Sheriff?" said a small, soft voice. "How do you feel?"

He raised his hand back to touch his throbbing head.

"What happened?" he asked. "The last thing I remember is having my head almost ripped off by one of those things."

He felt soft fingers pull his probing hand away from his bandaged head.

"You were fighting that thing, but it kept pounding your head against the car. Your gun fell in my lap. I didn't know what to do, so I grabbed the gun put it against the creature's head and pulled the trigger. That gun almost broke my wrists when it went off, but the thing let go of you and turned toward me."

She paused and Stark reached out for her hand.

"What happened, Betty? Tell me, please."

"I couldn't pull the hammer pack. I just didn't have the strength. I knew it would kill me and then kill you. Then I heard something move behind me as that thing reached for me. Your shotgun came across my shoulder and fired twice. I thought I had gone deaf."

"Benji? I completely forgot about that poor kid," said Stark, more to himself than to the girl. "Benji killed that thing."

"That's right, Sheriff. That poor kid came up from the floorboard firing as fast as he could chamber the rounds. The thing was damn hard to kill, but it finally stopped moving after he almost blew its' head apart. He also blew most of the left rear door off the car, so the thing fell out into the mud.

We drug you out from under the wheel; I slid into your place, started the car and drove it in here. You were bleeding badly and I didn't know what else to do so I pulled you out of the car and used my blouse to stop the bleeding. Now you lay still, Ben Stark, or I will have wasted my best blouse for nothing."

He smiled in the darkness as he felt her small fingers still holding his hand tightly and her breath against his cheek.

"Yes ma'am, I surely will lay still. But where's Benji?"

"He's at the front of the barn with your shotgun. He insisted that he needed to keep a watch for those things in case they came back. Now hush and go to sleep."

Sheila started to slide across the seat, but the stranger stopped her.

"You drive."

With a shrug she stepped back and let him slid across to the passenger door. Stepping into the truck, she started the motor and waited while he calmly leaned back and stretched.

"You sure that you want me to drive?" she asked as she put the truck into gear and let off the clutch.

"Probably better than my driving, I haven't been behind the wheel of a vehicle since before you were born." he said, his eyes scanning the darkness.

She spared him a glance as she fought the wheel to stay in the driveway.

"I hardly think you are that old."

He smiled a slow smile and returned her look.

"I am simply well preserved, youngster. I'm much older than I look."

She skidded to a stop near the service entrance of the old building. Almost before she was stopped, her passenger was out of the vehicle and across the courtyard to kneel beside a figure lying on the ground. The figure was dead; piano wire wrapped tightly around his neck. Sheila came to look over his shoulder.

"It's Dr. Peterson," she gasped, "Is---he dead?"

The stranger nodded slowly.

"Very dead."

Rising to his feet, the stranger appeared to grow before her eyes. Flexing his big hands, he walked quickly to the door and entered the old Mission. Sheila was left bending over the dead scientist, left only with the rain and the night.

CHAPTER TWENTY-FIVE

Slowly, placing his feet carefully, the big stranger prowled the corridors of the ancient building. Something about the atmosphere tugged at the gaps in his memory. There was something about the building that made him believe that he had been there before. He didn't feel that his last visit had been a pleasant one. His ears were straining for any sounds in the old building.

As he moved slowly along the corridor, it seemed as if the big man actually merged with the shadows that filled the long silent hallway. There was not a sound to mark his passage.

As he rounded the first corner in the long corridor, a scarlet clad figure almost collided with him. The stranger recovered first, with a sweep of his right arm, he sent the scarlet one reeling across the floor to crash into the wall. The sound of the combat brought several others of the scarlet raiders running. All were waving knives in their hands.

The first one to reach the stranger received a direct right, straight from his shoulder. The blow dropped him in his tracks just as if he'd been pole axed. The one behind him received a back fist that shattered his mouth and sent him sprawling back into his friends. Scarlet clad individuals went tumbling in all directions. The stranger followed up his advantage by kicking one in the face and grabbing another by the head and giving it a hard twist.

Sheila Bennett came running up in time to see the stranger sending the last of his attackers to dreamland. She skidded to a stop and surveyed the bodies sprawled over the hall.

"My god, there are eight men laying out here. You're not even breathing hard. I don't understand." She began. "One minute you're unconscious, suffering from a concussion and now you are fighting like the Incredible Hulk and not even breathing hard. It's impossible."

"Don't worry about it my dear, just accept." He swung around, his hawk like eyes probing the shadows. "Who else is here that should be here?"

"Dr. Bonner, and perhaps eight other scientists, and one monk are in that win," she pointed down the corridor to the left.

Silently, the big stranger almost flew down the silent, darkened hallway. Sheila had to almost run full out to keep up with him. She joined him as he bent over a figure dressed in jeans and a dark shirt, lying motionless on the floor. A pool of dark blood stained the floor near his head.

"Dr. Sonnerman." she identified, her voice husky. "What happened to him?"

"Throat cut." he responded simply, rising back to his feet. Swiftly, the big man went from cell to cell glancing inside.

"Empty," he mused, as if to himself. "Now, where would they take the rest of the scientists?"

"The Chapel, perhaps." suggested Sheila.

He looked at her with a smile.

"I am impressed, my dear. You are quick."

He turned and started toward the Chapel. Suddenly, he stopped, his head held high. Sheila came up to him and glanced around the dark silent building.

"What's wrong?" she demanded in a whisper.

"Are there any other women here?" he questioned as he slowly turned.

"Yes, Madam Sasha. Why?"

Without answering, the big man turned and rapidly moved down a side corridor. Sheila grimaced and followed after him. How does he know where things are in this old building, she wondered? These corridors are a maze and its' dark, but he acts like its' day light in here. Realizing he'd gone, she darted after him.

She found him flattened against the wall outside one of the empty cells in a long unused wing of the Mission. From inside the room, she could hear the sound of a struggle.

"No, get away from me!" shrieked a female voice.

"That's Madame Sasha." identified Sheila, tugging at his sleeve.

He smiled down at her for a moment; then the smile vanished, replaced by a stern face.

"Wait here." he ordered, moving toward the doorway.

As he stood in the doorway and pushed the door open, he could see that a candle fully illuminated the room. A rather attractive older woman was cowering back in the far corner of the room as two scarlet clad men advanced on her, their arms spread wide. Her blouse had been ripped from her body; pieces of it littered the floor.

Silently, he advanced behind the two would be rapists. At the last moment, one of them sensed him and spun around, a knife held in one hand. Before he could use it, the big man swatted him out of the way with a languid backhand. A rapid sidekick dropped the second rapist. Madame Sasha slumped to the floor, sobbing quietly to herself. Sheila ran forward to wrap her arms around the sobbing psychic.

"Sasha, did they hurt you?" she asked gently.

"No----but they were planning to do terrible things to me. I could sense their thoughts." she responded as she wiped the tears from her eyes.

Realizing that she was on the floor, she struggled to regain her feet, but froze when the big man came forward to take her arm and help her up. She backed against the wall, her eyes locked to his, her breathing slowed almost to nothing.

"Age, I sense unbelievable age and sadness."

She paused and looked at him with wide-eyed shock.

"You are one who has walked for eternity. You are the blessed one spoke of in legend."

Slowly she raised both hands and placed them on his head. Sheila gasped as the big man; so powerful in vanquishing his enemies fell to the floor limply. Madame Sasha knelt beside him, pacing both hands upon his forehead. For a long moment she knelt over the fallen man, who lay so still and limp, Sheila thought that he was dead. Surprisingly, she felt a deep sense of loss. Suddenly, he moved, one hand coming up to grasp Madam Sasha's arm.

Slowly, still clutching her arm, the fallen hero pulled himself to his feet.

Releasing his grip on her arm, the man stepped back and favored her with a sad glance.

"My thanks for your help, wise one. But I am not blessed, wise woman, but cursed. You two wait here. I'll go free the rest."

He moved so rapidly that he seemed to disappear before their very eyes. He was gone.

Damn!" exclaimed Sheila, "I wish he would quit doing that."

Fred Santos was sitting very quietly in his kitchen, lost in the shadows as he had let the fire burn down in the hearth. He found that he was missing Ringo more than he wanted to let anyone know. Add to that his nerves were so jumpy that he had strapped on his old .44. It was his intent to just drink coffee until the storm was over. He had actually begun to get drowsy when he caught sight of movement outside his kitchen window.

Springing to his feet, Santos trotted over to peer out the steamy window. If it was Ringo coming back, he wanted to be ready to greet his old friend. He certainly intended to give him a piece of his mind for scaring the hell out of him. To his surprise, he saw nothing. But he was certain that he had seen movement.

He had started back toward his chair when he heard the rasp of the doorknob as it slowly turned. Certainly Ringo had every right to come and go as he wanted, but there would have been no need for his old friend to sneak about. He suddenly had a feeling that it wasn't his old friend. Drawing the old .44, Santos moved just inside the passageway to the store, slowly cocked back the hammer and waited. His caution was well justified, for he had begun to believe that perhaps all was not as it should be this night.

With the sound of rushing feet, the back door slammed back against the wall and several scarlet clad figures came charging into the kitchen, waving knives and screaming insanely. They halted in confusion when they found the kitchen empty.

"Where'd that old coot go?" demanded the leader, "I know I saw him sitting in that chair when I looked in the window just now."

For a second the intruders milled around the kitchen in confusion. It seemed to throw their plans off to not find Santos where they had expected to see him. Taking a deep breath, Santos stepped out of the passageway, .44 ready.

"I'm right here assholes!" he barked as he began to fan the hammer of the old weapon.

The big .44 rounds made some major holes in the pretty scarlet outfits that his attackers were wearing. Three died on the kitchen floor from gunshot wounds. Overcome with rage at the invasion of his home, Santos waded into the survivors, swinging the old handgun like a club. Those that could, ran for the backdoor and safety, to become jammed in the doorway as they all tried to exit at once. Santos scooped up a 9 mm automatic pistol that one of them had dropped and emptied the 14 round magazine into the scarlet clad figures massed struggling in his doorway. Soon they were struggling no more.

"That'll teach those goddamn outsiders to leave the last of the Santos brothers alone in the future." he growled to himself as he opened the loading gate of the old .44 and began to feed more of the big rounds into the chambers.

"Reckon I'll just wander outside and see if there's any more of these varmints around." he muttered as he strode out the back door, not caring that he walked on still warm bodies in the process.

Soon, only the sound of the rain and the wind could be heard in the room, as the door swung slowly open on its hinges. Fred Santos, the last of the fighting Santos Brothers, was on the hunt.

In the main Chapel of the Old Mission, Dr. Bonner and the rest of his team of researchers were lined up in front of the altar, their hands held high above their heads. Numerous torches held by a number of scarlet clad figures that lined the walls, facing toward the front entrance, brightly lighted the room. Two of the scarlet ones held the scientists at gunpoint while the rest ran toward the front of the building, to open the main gates of the Mission Compound. Once the gates were open those that had gathered inside the outer yard formed two lines, one on either side of the entrance. They silently stood at attention and waited.

The stranger stood just inside of the passage, watching the activity in the Chapel. He took his eyes off the lit room only when Sheila and Madame Sasha came up behind him. Sheila pushed by him and peered around the door facing, surveying the room.

"My god, there must be fifty of those goons in that room. Where did they come from?"

His dark eyes gleaming in the torchlight, he shrugged.

"Where they came from isn't important. It's what to do with them that's the question."

A sudden flurry of activity at the front of the Chapel caused the torchbearers to crowd toward the activity. A gleaming Rolls Royce pulled up before the main entrance, the rain beat down even heavier. Two of those waiting rushed forward to open the rear passenger door for the ones inside the car to exit. The two guards moved to the side so that they could both watch the activity at the entrance and also watch their captives.

Taking advantage of the confusion, the stranger slid forward into the Chapel, making no sound. He silently went up behind the two guards, his feet making absolutely no sound as he moved. His eyes met those of Dr. Bonner, but a finger to his lips cautioned the scientists to stay silence.

In a movement too rapid for Sheila's eyes to follow, his hands flashed up to grab each of the guards by their hair and slammed their heads together. Both crumpled to the floor, their weapons falling from limp hands.

"Quickly," he hissed at the stunned scientists, "Follow Sheila. Get out of here as quickly as you can."

No one moved until they saw Sheila wave to them, but then they almost ran over each other to get out of the Chapel. She led them rapidly down the dark corridor toward the courtyard where she had parked her truck when she noticed the stranger was not with them. She stopped in her tracks.

"Where did he go?"

"Who?" asked Dr. Bonner looking around in confusion.

"The big man that saved you; why isn't he with us?"

"He stayed back there," responded one of the others, pointing back toward the Chapel.

"I've got to go back," said Sheila, starting back down the corridor.

Dr. Bonner grabbed her by the arm.

"Sheila, it's too dangerous. Those people are killers."

"But he's back there by himself. I have to help him," she protested, trying to pull away from the older man.

Dr. Bonner pulled on her arm.

"My dear, there is nothing that you nor we can do. We aren't armed, they are. There is absolutely nothing we can do. Even your friend told us to get away."

She stood silently for a few seconds and then slowly she turned back toward the courtyard where her truck was parked. Only a few saw her tears reflected in the flickering torchlight.

"We're going to town to get help and then coming back!" she stated flatly.

The others followed her out into the night.

Fred Santos moved quickly from shadow to shadow as he made his way along the north side of the main street of El Noche. He saw absolutely nothing moving along the storm lashed streets. He crouched down in the alley, at the edge of the trading post, waiting for someone to show himself. Santos was about to decide that his idea had been a mistake when he saw two of those scarlet robed figures striding down the street, forcing the

Doctor and his sister, Emily, before them, through the rain toward the Cafe. He started to move slowly in their wake, trying to stay out of sight as he could see two more of the scarlet robes waiting on the porch outside the café doors.

In fact, he was so concerned with following the Doctor and his sister, that he didn't pay enough attention to his own surroundings. He froze when he felt a gun barrel pock him in the ribs.

"Freeze old man!" ordered a high-pitched voice. "Take one more move and I'll blow you in half."

"Old man?" questioned Santos, his temper starting to rise.

Slowly he turned around to find that his captor was a pimply-faced kid in his early twenties, all dressed up in one of those fancy red robes. Fred's old eyes looked the kid up and down slowly.

"You called me an old man?" he demanded.

The young man smirked and poked the old man in the ribs with his rifle again. "Move it, grandpa or I'll drop you like a bad habit."

The last insult was too much for the old man. He grabbed the rifle barrel with his left hand, jerked the kid close and slammed his right elbow into the kid's defenseless jaw. The gunman crumpled to the wet ground.

"Thanks for the rifle, sonny." said Santos moving off into the night.

Simon Dakkar exited the Rolls Royce and strolled grandly through the front entrance of the Monastery. Close behind him were Julia and two larger figures that served as his bodyguards. He felt full of the master's power in this moment of his triumph.

His senior acolyte nodded low before him, before rising to walk at his side.

"Master, we have captured the interlopers as you ordered. The Master's House is free of the vermin."

"Excellent, I am pleased with your work thus far. Did you find Miss Bennett?" he said to his aide, nodding to the honor guard that lined his way down the aisle.

"No, Lord. The woman was not among them. She seems to have disappeared."

Dakkar frowned and turned his eyes toward his subordinate.

"This is not good. If we do not find her, all may be for naught."

The acolyte cringed under the glare of his superior but stood his ground.

"However, in searching the room that was hers, we did find this." he said raising his right hand to show that he was holding a golden disk dangling from a chain.

Immediately, Dakkar's stern expression changed to one of reverence.

"The disk? You found it."

He took it into his large hands and caressed it slowly.

"You are to be complemented. You have given me the final key to the Master's prison."

Suddenly a thought struck him.

"The scientists: where are they being held?"

"At the altar, Lord." replied the Acolyte, turning to point toward the rear of the Chapel. Suddenly, his smile faded as he glanced toward the altar and saw that instead of the captured scientists, two of his guards were propped against the altar itself. Both were obviously dead.

Simon Dakkar stood and surveyed the scene in front of him. His face was expressionless, his eyes flat and dead. Spinning, Dakkar brought his right hand back in a blurring motion to slam into the side of his senior acolyte's head. The smaller man fell where he stood. Dakkar continued on down the aisle to stop before the two dead guards.

"Very professional," he complemented. "Whoever did this is a real pro. He will regret interfering in something he has no right to be involved in."

Slowly he turned and motioned to his two bodyguards.

"Find the one that did this! Kill him!" he ordered.

Silently, the two robed figures walked up and stood, almost

sniffing the air around the dead bodies, before they both turned and trotted off across the Chapel into the dark corridor that led to the sleeping cells. Dakkar stepped up to the altar and bowed his head in prayer to his infernal Lord. Leaning forward, he placed his thumb against a darker spot on the back of the altar and applied pressure. The top of the altar pivoted to reveal an opening into which he dropped the golden disk. A low hum began to penetrate the room. He returned to his prayers.

Asmodeus was imprisoned in a massive force field powered by the magnetic field of the earth itself. There were seven keys to the lock on the prison, the golden disk being the seventh and the most powerful. The golden disk worked as a rod would in a nuclear reactor, it caused the force field that kept Asmodeus sealed in his prison to power down. In the weakened state, Asmodeus would have enough power to force his way through and return to the surface world.

Dakkar was disturbed from his devotions by the sound of a body thudding against one of the pews to his rear. Looking around, he saw the second of his bodyguards come sailing through the doorway to slam into the pews. Both had been thrown with incredible force. For a moment, he knelt silently, unable to believe his eyes.

Rising to his feet, Dakkar motioned to several of his men standing nearby.

"Whoever that is kill him. He disturbs me," he snapped.

Responding with enthusiasm, the members of the Order rushed toward the doorway, weapons at the ready. Before his eyes, a burst of energy slammed into the group, scattering them in all directions. Dakkar tossed his topcoat into a nearby pew and drew himself to his full height. Raising his right hand, he concentrated, concentrating intently on his hand. A blue glow appeared to clover his hand and then a burst of blue flame leaped from his hand to vanish into the dark corridor. To his utter shock his energy bolt was reflected back into the room, to just barely miss his head.

"Who's there!" he demanded, "I, Voice of The Infernal Master, command you to show yourself."

"Just me, Simon." came a soft voice from the darkness. "Still worshipping that filth, I see."

From the darkness of the corridor stepped the blonde stranger, his eyes glowing with an internal power he had not shown before. Through rips in his prison shirt, the rippling muscles of the man could be seen, radiating physical strength.

"You!" breathed Simon Dakkar, backing up a step, "But I killed you two hundred years ago. I saw you die."

Sadly it seemed, the blonde stranger slowly shook his head.

"No, Simon, you didn't kill me physically, though you might as well have done so. You and your renegades took the only woman I have loved in all the many thousands of centuries I have been cursed to walk this dreary, lonely world. Being alone is another type of death, I have found. For that alone I will punish you and your attempt to free the filth that represents all that is evil."

Simon raised his cane and pointed it at the blonde.

"Well, then I'll kill you now." he cursed as he called upon the full power of Asmodeus to send a bolt of raw energy flying across the room toward the big stranger.

The bolt of energy hit with a blinding flash and a loud explosion. Those of the Order who were standing too close were sent flying across the room. Even Dakkar, himself, was staggered by the very force he had released. Nothing could have survived a direct hit from so much of the Master's infernal power. When Dakkar's eyes cleared, the stranger was gone.

"At last!" declared Dakkar throwing his arms wide, "I've finally killed that bastard. The Ancient Prince will reward me with great riches. There is nothing to stand in the way of the Master conquering the world as is his right."

"Ah, Simon, my old friend, you have always been too optimistic." came a soft voice from behind him.

Dakkar spun around to see the blonde stranger sitting comfortably on the altar, dangling the golden disk from his big right hand. The hum that had previously filled the room had stopped. Dakkar had not noticed the absence of the hum in the aftermath of the energy explosion. His reptile-like eyes were riveted on the golden disk held easily in the big man's hand. That disk was the one key he had not been able to obtain in the thousands of years he had searched for a way to free his Master. With a roar, the formerly dapper Dakkar lunged toward the stranger, fingers outstretched like talons. Almost instantly, he found himself flying through the air as the stranger back handed him with his left hand.

Bounding back to his feet, Dakkar rushed toward his foe who stood easily on the altar steps, seemingly waiting for his foe to approach. At the last second, the big man leapt into the air and slammed his right foot into Dakkar's chest, sending him tumbling through the air. He crashed into the pews about half way down the Chapel.

While everyone else had been preoccupied, Julia had worked her way to the rear of the altar area. Her fingers curled like claws, Julia hissed and launched herself toward the big man. Just before she had landed on his back, he simply wasn't there; she crashed to the floor on her stomach, the breath knocked from her deadly body. Before she could regain her feet, she was picked up by the back of her robe and tossed the length of the room to crash into a group of Scarlet Robes that had gathered for a rush to try and overpower the big man.

Julia sprang to her feet as quick as a cat. Hissing, she came rushing down the aisle, her ceremonial knife clutched in her hand. With an annoyed frown, the big man grabbed the candelabra from the altar and sent it spinning toward the woman. The base of the metal missile caught her between her almond eyes. She fell limply to the floor.

Staggering to his feet, Dakkar felt his magically enhanced power draining away as the seventh lock renewed itself and his infernal Master was slowly resealed in his eternal prison. Without the golden disk, the final security device holding Asmodeus in eternal bondage could not be released, Asmodeus was still trapped. The first six locks were open, so Asmodeus could see and influence happenings on the earth's surface, but he could not take a direct hand. The seventh lock had been the strongest failsafe device that could be devised by the Ancient Gods to hold their greatest threat in bondage. The ancient world grid began to return to a condition of full power.

”You think you are so good, don't you.” Dakkar spat at his foe, “Well, these same humans that you try so hard to protect are the ones that cracked open the Master's prison with their probing and prying into secrets that are not rightfully theirs.

“When they set off the atomic bomb here, it was they that cracked the walls of his prison. It was they who give such as me the power to work our magic. How can you serve such beings? You and I are brothers, how can you serve those that even over threw the ancient gods from which we both are descended.”

The big man shrugged.

“I don't know, Simon. I only know that my father placed me on this earth with a mission. I have to try and help those that are oppressed, to protect them from your so-called master. I only know that whatever side you are on, I have no choice but to be on the other side.”

Dakkar straightened his rumpled white suit and took the cane that one of his few remaining assistants offered him. He slowly walked to the center of the aisle to stand for a moment facing the big man.

“It is too bad that we could not be truly brothers. I, too, am all alone on this dreary world. All of my blood lies buried in the sands of time. Only you and I walk the land. No matter how hard I try to form attachments, they eventually fail due to the frail nature of these animals. I am positive that you have had the same problem.”

He studied the big man through hooded eyes.

“The time for opening the prison gates has passed. However, there will be other opportunities to free my Master, other times and other battles. Even now, as a last act, the Master has released the Piasa and the horned ones. Immortal though you might be, I do not believe that even you can survive those?

“Remember, it was only one of the Piasa that destroyed the entire tribe of the Anasazi you lived with those centuries ago. You couldn't stand against the Master's creatures then and you can't now. Until I see you again farewell, my friend.”

Flinging out his hand, Dakkar caused the candles in the room to be immediately extinguished, returning the room to pitch blackness. Turning, Dakkar ran out the front entrance and dove into the safety of his waiting Rolls Royce. Smoothly the car pulled away from the Old Mission. His three remaining followers charged forward to cover their leader's escape. Though the room was pitch black, their target grabbed the first attacker and easily tossed him the length of the Chapel. The other two were quickly dispatched with a sidekick and a hard right fist.

The stranger arrived at the entrance in time to see the taillights of the automobile disappear into the night. When Dakkar's car had disappeared into the storm, the big man pulled the chain over his head, the gold disk resting on his chest. He slowly walked the length of the aisle, stepping over the bodies that littered the way, to stand before the altar."

"Asmodeus!" he called across the empty chapel, "I am here! Face me if you dare."

The ancient building shook as the infernal beast raged in his underground prison. The very altar itself began to glow with the radiated power of the demon.

"My father sent me to be a guardian to such as you," continued the challenger, "He never wanted you to be able to walk among the people of the world again. I swear that I shall spend my days carrying out his wishes. Fight me if you dare."

Turning his back on the altar of the most infernal Asmodeus, the stranger walked slowly up the aisle, lost in thought.

"This is not like you, Simon, to give up so easily. What are you planning?" he wondered aloud as he stepped into the stormy night. Slowly, he walked away from the Mission, down the long road toward the Devil's Hill cut. As he walked, an Indian who came silently from the darkness suddenly joined him.

"I have waited so many years, my friend. Do you remember me now?"

The big stranger smiled and shrugged.

"I remember. I remember everything. I remember that I wanted to die when I lost her, but the gods denied me even that. So I did the next best thing, I mentally died. Then-----"

"Then her essence woke you from your private hell?" asked the Indian softly.

He took a deep breath and sighed, his face lined with pain.

"It was her, my friend, I have no doubt it was her. She looked just as she did the day that I first met her. But she didn't know me. To see her and not be able to touch her is torture."

"You have always been too quick to judge, my friend. Give her time. If you are meant to be together, then she will remember," cautioned the Indian, glancing up as a dark shape crossed above them heading toward the town.

As one, both spun at the sound of a quiet footstep behind them. A dark robed figure stood at the corner of the Mission.

"You are the promised one, aren't you?" came a soft voice.

The big man stood silently, studying the dark robed figure. Finally, he answered.

"I don't know about being the promised one, but I am a foe of the one who lives beneath this building."

"You are the guardian of this place?" questioned the Indian.

The unseen figure nodded, his features shadowed by the looming building.

"I have been here for more than sixty years. I swore an oath that I would remain here until I either rescued my love or killed the one that took her. In those years I have come to be able to sense the presence of the hellish creatures that serve the evil one. Many of them have left this doorway to hell, this night, and headed for the town below."

"Then I would suggest that we pay a visit to the village," suggested the Indian. Almost before the eyes of the guardian, the two vanished into the night.

PART IV

THE TOWN

CHAPTER TWENTY-SIX

The Sheriff pulled himself into a sitting position. Betty had finally fallen asleep, curled up in the hay beside him. He almost lay back down as his head began to throb like a big bass drum. Rolling to the side, the Sheriff pulled himself to his knees. Slowly, he fought his way to his feet, swaying slightly as the world spun around him.

He tensed as he felt hands grab him.

"What are doing on your feet!" demanded Betty McNabb, her lovely face dark with anger. "You ought to be flat on your back for a good many days to come."

Forcing himself to stand straight, the Sheriff turned and smiled down at the girl.

"Betty, I have a town depending on me for protection. With those things running around out there, I can't very well lay here in the hay safe and warm." he paused and smiled even wider, "much as I certainly want to."

Betty blushed a deep pink and her anger subsided.

"Well, at least don't strain yourself until we can get the Doctor to look at those head wounds. They look serious to me."

"Yes ma'am." he said as he walked slowly toward his car. "Benji, where are you?"

"Here, sir" came the answer from the partially opened barn door.

"Get in the car, son. Be sure and keep that shotgun ready," he said, turning to Betty. "Girl, you sit in the middle."

Everyone in place, Stark started the car and slowly backed out into the storm.

The scarlet robed figures stood at attention outside the doors to the Café, automatic weapons at port arms. They kept their cowls pulled up to shield their faces from the rain, but their eyes never left the street. Fred Santos stood inside the deep set entrance to the abandoned feed store and peered out at the guards. He wondered what they were guarding.

His eyes were drawn to the street as a powerful fancy motorcar pulled up before the café. The two guards ran down the steps to open the rear car door. A big, well-dressed man exited the car and ran up the steps, the café doors opened as he reached the porch and he entered. The guards returned to their positions on either side of the door.

Well, that's interesting, thought Santos. Obviously, the new arrival was the big shot. Those guards had acted like he was a king or something. He had to get those guards out of the way before the big shot did something that they would all regret. He had about made up his mind to move in on the guards when he spotted movement in the alley beside the Café. Straining his eyes, he was able to make out that an old blanket covered Indian stood just out of sight of the guards. With a shock, he realized that it was Ringo's blanket that he was watching.

Even as he watched, the bent over Indian stepped out into plain view of the guards. Both spun and leveled their weapons at the blanket-covered figure. He couldn't hear what the guards said, but he saw Ringo raise his hands and walk slowly up the steps and into the Café. One of the guards entered behind him. The second took up a position directly in front of the doors.

Inside the café, there were numerous candles lit, giving as much illumination as if the electricity was back on. Simon Dakkar was sitting in a chair in front of the now roaring fire, Mace Runnels stood quietly behind him. The remaining customers were lined up against the bar.

"Good people, I am sure that you realize that something unusual is going on in this fine valley of yours. Well if that's what you thought, then you are quite right."

"Well speak up, young man." demanded Minnie Foster in her own inimitable way. "What is going on here? Who are these extremely rude people with guns?"

"Young man?" mused Dakkar, "If only that was true, woman. Well, no matter. There are things to be done.

"Unlike you Christians, who worship a dead god, I worship Asmodeus, the eternal infernal god of evil. He lies imprisoned near here, as he has been since before the beginnings of time. I, we, came to free him this night, but we were thwarted in our attempts to free our Master by a creature that had no business living."

"Heathen!" snapped Minnie Foster.

"Our Master hungers," continued Dakkar as if there had been no interruptions. "He must be fed. Since we could not free him tonight, we are therefore charged with insuring that he is fed. We have chosen you humans to be his food. We can take you to him still living or we can kill you as long as we have you to him within an hour."

Dakkar stopped to look up at Runnels as a pounding was heard at the rear door of the Café. Wordlessly, the killer crossed the room to unlock the heavy rear door. A group of individuals, thoroughly soaked to the skin came dashing inside to crowd before the fire. Dakkar had moved into the shadows as they milled about the room. Finally he stepped back into the light.

"Well Miss Bennett, Dr. Bonner, so good of you to join us." he purred.

Sheila Bennett's face turned as white as a sheet and she turned to run. She ran directly into the slight Mace Runnels as she ran for the door. He grabbed her wrists and held them tightly in one hand.

"What is the meaning of this?" demanded Dr. Bonner.

Dakkar resumed his seat and leaned on his cane.

"Quite simple Dr. Bonner, you and your associates, with the exception of the lovely Miss Bennett are to be sacrifices to my infernal Master."

He stopped in his explanation as the front door opened and the guard herded a new prisoner inside. The Indian stood silently, his blanket still clutched about him in the center of the room, his dark eyes riveted in Dakkar's direction. He totally ignored the guard when he nudged his rifle into the Indian's back.

"Move your ass, Indian! Get over against the bar with the others," snapped the guard.

Instead of moving, the Indian slowly straightened to his full height, allowing the soggy blanket to fall to the floor. He turned his head, looked over his right shoulder and favored the guard with a flat stare. Certain of the protection of his master and supremely arrogant in his ability to intimidate the citizens, the guard reversed his weapon and rammed the stock into the Indian's back. To his surprise, the Indian never moved nor changed expression.

The startled guard backed up a step as the Indian whirled and backhanded the guard across the face. The scarlet figure was knocked totally off his feet to hit the floor solidly on his back. Everyone in the room froze, their eyes held by the big Indian. The Indian turned to face Dakkar, the only one who had not moved throughout the entire performance.

"Who are you, Indian?" he asked quietly.

"I know you, Indian!" interrupted Runnels, stepping up to stand beside his superior.

"I being you a message, evil one." stated the Indian, folding his arms and pointedly ignoring the killer.

"A message?" repeated Dakkar, raising one eyebrow, raising one hand to silence Runnels.

"I am to tell you that you will not win. You will suffer another great defeat this night."

Dakkar smiled widely, his look that of a feral animal.

"And who would dare to have sent me such a message?" he purred, eyes narrowed.

"He who must be obeyed sent me."

"And who is that, Indian?" asked Dakkar.

"Me!" answered a deep voice from behind them.

CHAPTER TWENTY-SEVEN

Santos finally decided to make his move. Raising his stolen rifle, he sighted in on the single guard. Slowly, he tightened his finger on the trigger until he fired the single shot. The guard slammed back against the wall and fell limply forward. As he moved from his place toward the Café building, Santos heard a racing engine coming from the direction of Devil's Hill. Walking to the edge of the wide porch, Santos strained his eyes and finally recognized the Sheriff's car racing toward the center of town. Waving his arms wildly, he flagged down the battered patrol car.

"What's the problem, Fred?" demanded the bandaged Sheriff, as Sheila cranked down the passenger window.

"Some crazies have taken over the town, got most of the town's people locked up in the café over there."

Santos suddenly realized that the car was almost a complete wreck and he saw a lot of dried blood on the front of the Sheriff's uniform jacket.

"Damn, Ben, what happened to you?"

"Fred, you wouldn't believe me if I told you. How many people we got that can use guns?"

"I'm afraid that I'm the only one that ain't locked up inside that place."

Further conversation was halted as a scarlet clad body came crashing through the front doors of the café to roll into the muddy street.

"You!" gasped Sheila Bennett ceasing her struggles.

Dakkar sprang to his feet as he saw the dripping figure standing just inside the rear door.

"Damn you for your interference. There are rules to our encounters. You know that you are forbidden to interfere with the minions of my Master. You, like I, are forbidden to interfere with the creatures which in habit this planet."

"I'm changing the rules," rumbled the figure, "I will fight you every step of the way."

Suddenly Dakkar grinned, "Oh, you'll fight all right, but not with me."

From the darkness outside the rear door, a huge red skinned figure charged through the door to wrap his massive arms around the stranger. A gang of scarlet clad men followed in his wake. With a mighty roar, the giant creature lifted the blonde from his feet. Taking advantage of the confusion, Runnels flung his prisoner aside, pulled a knife from his belt and dove at the still motionless Indian. The battle was on.

With a surge of power, the blonde broke the giant's bear hug. Turning slightly, the blonde drove his right elbow into the solar plexus of the giant, doubling him over. The Indian and Runnels were standing toe to toe, slugging it out. The scarlet figures swarmed over everyone as Dakkar darted out the rear door.

Minnie Foster was the first of the hostages to react. She grabbed a partially empty bottle from the bar and slammed it down on the head of the first of the scarlet attackers. Following her example, the others began to fight back. In just a few minutes, there were bodies bouncing off walls and furniture all over the café.

One of the raiders made the mistake of jumping on the back of the Indian fighting with Runnels. The Indian paid absolutely no attention to the man clinging to his back, but continued to trade punches with Runnels. He could sense that there was something different about Runnels. There was a difference in his aura than when they fought in the storm. Putting all his power into one punch, he slammed Runnels head over heels across the room. Grabbing the man on his back by the top of his head, he peeled him off and literally tossed him across the room to crash through the front doors out into the storm.

When the Indian went to aide his friend, he found that the big blonde had made short work of the giant that had attacked him. The situation seemed to be well in hand, so it was time for them to leave. They started for the rear door when a voice called to them.

"Freeze, you two!"

Turning, they saw that the Sheriff was standing in the shattered doorway, pointing a riot shotgun at them. From the expression on his face, it was clear that he would not hesitate to pull the trigger. Fred Santos stood just behind him, his old .44 cocked and ready to fire.

"You are mistaken, Sheriff." offered the blonde. "We are not your enemies."

"Well, maybe you are and maybe you're not, but I don't know who you are and until I do you ain't going anywhere."

"Ben Stark, you stop that foolishness and come arrest this white trash." ordered Minnie Foster, walking over to stand in front of his weapon. "These boys came to help and don't you go treating them like criminals."

"Miss Minnie, I gotta do my job and right now that's to arrest anyone I don't know until I can get to the bottom of this mess. Hey, where'd they go?"

Ben Stark ran across the room to peer out the back door, but the two had vanished into the night. He leaned tiredly against the doorframe and rubbed his sore eyes. He was so tired. Glancing up, he noticed that the night was a little lighter, dawn was near. The long night was over.

CHAPTER TWENTY-EIGHT

The clean-up was slow and solemn. Ben Stark deputized many of the able bodied men and began a search for survivors. The dead town people numbered more than a score; many of the buildings had been vandalized. The scarlet raiders were found scattered around the town, most with broken jaws or with huge lumps on their heads.

Sheriff Ben Stark recovered, nursed back to health by Betty McNabb. His wounds were serious, but not fatal. Their wedding day was the day after he was returned to full duty.

Fred Santos had been sitting ready when the raiders had stormed his store. Santos lived up to his self-description, as a man who would not be removed. Over fifteen of the raiders were found in the front of the store. Santos, himself, was hit four times. He had walked over to seek medical attention and found that the raiders were in the Doctor's house. His old .44 had a real work out that day. The Doctor's sister was visiting from Dallas; she thought he was a real hero. Folks said that it looked like there might be a Mrs. Santos soon.

Old Ringo, who had been a fixture in the town as long as anyone could remember, was never seen again. It was assumed that the raiders killed him. Fred Santos just smiled when anyone asked about the old Indian.

The F.B.I. swarmed over the old town when the prison van was found wrecked on the hill above the town. They had been searching for their agent and his prisoner since a scheduled telephone contact had not taken place. Kramer was given a military funeral, as befitted someone who died in the line of duty. Law enforcement agencies in a dozen countries went on alert, looking for Runnels. Number 35 was looked for in the general area and then forgotten, after all, he really had no record that could be found. They didn't even know his name.

Only one person seemed to care what happened to Number 35. Sheila Bennett had searched the area around the town a dozen times looking for some sign of the mysterious man she had rescued. She had also searched for miles around the old Mission looking for the one man she could not forget. She never found him.

Amanda Bennett was assumed to have died in the storm. Her car was found nose down in one of the flooded arroyos, the door open, and the body gone. As soon as communication was re-established with the outside world, Sheila Bennett also found out that her father had died recently, so her grief was double. She was now alone in the world, though her double inheritance would make her independently wealthy.

Madame Sasha and Dr. Bonner became rather close during the aftermath and were generally always together.

The unusual storm had gradually petered itself out over the next few days, but after that battle in the town, the unusual force was missing from the wind.

Sheila had forgotten her birthday was coming, but Dr. Bonner had remembered. Partially because of her birthday and partially to take her mind off her grief, Dr. Bonner took her and Madame Sasha to the Double Eagle Restaurant in Mesilla, New Mexico for a quiet dinner. The building and some of its furnishings dated back to the late 1700's.

The dinner had been excellent, the company charming. She had gradually relaxed under the charm of the older man. However, over wine, she had fallen into a thoughtful mood.

"You miss him don't you?" asked the older man, sipping from his glass.

"Who?" she asked trying to appear puzzled.

Bonner smiled slowly and glanced around the room.

"My dear, I may be old, but I am not stupid. You are still thinking about the big blonde man. As well you might, he saved us all."

She had at first nodded and then shook her head.

"Yes I guess I am, I mean no, I mean that I don't know what I mean." She paused searching for the words. "There was something about him that I can't forget. It's like I knew him, but didn't realize that I knew him until after I lost him."

Madame Sasha smiled knowingly.

"You realize that your destinies are joined."

Before Sheila could respond, Dr, Bonner smiled and then reached across the table to take her hand.

"Come with me, my dear. There is something I wish to show you."

Without a word, he led her across the dining room to a set of double doors. He opened one of the doors and led her into another empty dining room. He gently pulled the door shut behind him.

"This room was used as many things over the years. This was the home of the governor at one time. Many have lived here and I believe that each of them left something behind. There is something I wish to show you."

He came to a stop before a large oil painting on the wall. She stopped beside him and looked up at the painting. She started to turn away and then looked again, her surprise evident on her lovely face. The woman in the painting was her double. Moving closer, she squinted to read the nameplate.

"Donna Maria Dominguez Rogelio, daughter of the Governor and her husband, Don Diego Rogelio."

She looked back at the portrait and this time her eyes really bugged out; she swayed on her feet supported only by the arms of Dr. Bonner.

"Professor, that man, his face, it's the same man I pulled out of the van. It's him."

Silently, Dr. Bonner led her slowly back toward the dining room.

Madame Sasha hadn't moved, but sat silently, a small smile on her face. Sheila dropped into her chair and turned a puzzled face toward the older woman.

"I just saw---"

"Yes, my dear, he came across the years to save his true love. I have no proof, but I firmly believe that he came at a time that you needed him. It's my belief that he will never be far from you."

Sheila was so overwhelmed by what she had seen that she never noticed the two well-dressed men at a table near the door as she was led back to her own table. One of the two at the other table was a big blonde man and the other, a middle-aged man who appeared to have some American Indian blood.

When Dr. Bonner's eyes happened to meet those of the blonde man, the blonde raised his glass in a toast, to which Dr. Bonner inclined his head, a slight smile creasing his worn face. Madame Sasha favored him with a look that spoke volumes.

Leaving the funds for the check on the table, the blonde and his friend walked out into the ever-deepening night, the door closed behind them.

THE END: UNTIL NEXT TIME